PERCHANCE
a LIFE

PERCHANCE
a LIFE

stories, capriccios *&* an essay

Christine de Lailhacar

RHINE
HUDSON
BOOKS

This book is a work of fiction. Any reference to real people, events, establishments or locales are intended only to provide a sense of authenticity and are used fictitiously. All other characters, incidents, locales, and dialogue are drawn from the author's imagination and are not to be construed as real.

ISBN: 978-0-578-71742-5

Publisher: Rhine-Hudson Books
Contact: cdelailhacar@aol.com
Website: http://cdelailhacar.ag-sites.net/index.htm

Book Design: wordsintheworks.com

For

Marianne, Alix, and Zoé

Table of Contents

Avant Propos

*M*emories crystallize into stories, fiction pointing back to an initial trigger: a lived moment, more often an intensely felt impression.

The significance of any outside "action" lies in its imprint on the mind. If some of the pieces united in this book can be considered "action-packed" it is not in the sense of the reader's compulsion to learn what "happens" on the next page. It is not about the "smoking gun"—only about the smoke and the vibrations it causes in the mind.

It is impossible to pigeonhole vibrations, which is why these prose pieces can only be divided into non-categories, tangents to *short stories, capriccios,* and *personal essays,* as they emerge from pen strokes like the brush strokes of impressionists which, together, form a vision—*Perchance a Life.*

Selfies

$\mathcal{W}$ith nothing better to do during this visit to my mother's ramshackle French château, I am getting lost in contemplation of all my "forebears" whose portraits have invaded like flies every surface of parlour and library.

My multi-divorced mother's obsession with noble lineage has here brought together a motley crowd of totally non-related "relatives." Who's that grim-looking American general—or admiral?—decorated like a Christmas tree?

Next to him an old woman in black, visibly of modest origin and totally lost among this vanity fair; behind her, a dull looking teenager with what seems, even on the black and white picture, mousy-brown hair—oh, pardon, that's my mother, Gretel, before she reinvented herself as Lucrezia, kind of Renaissance femme fatale, "Venetian blonde" because Botticelli did not come up with a more sensuous hair colour for his Florentine Venuses.

At the edge of the marble plate of the mantelpiece, an elderly man in a striped apron is smiling in front of a barrel inscribed "Forster Ungeheuer, 1933" by which I know he was German, possibly my grand-father, and that the barrel contained the prestigious Rhenish Millésime 1933, the "Monster" fit to celebrate the beginning of the Thousand-Year Reich.

That one seems to be the feathered helmet of an American Grand Master of Free Masons and over there is a dabber Russian World War II officer and a faded picture of two German WWI soldiers in which I recognize my paternal great- grandfather and very young grandfather. Even more faded are three officers with those odd Prussian pointed helmets. And many ladies, so full of self-importance... After all, give credit where credit is due: in her way, my mother has some merit. Who would remember these individuals today had she not invited them to her house in order to borrow their self-attributed importance for the enhancement of her own? But who cares?

The rare visitors to this place in the backwoods of northern France don't have a clue of what these faded faces represent. Inconsequential. Even Lucrezia's present life is not the logical sequel to the one(s) she led before, not some Merry Widow version. Apparently, she prefers her own, photo-doctored past to a prosaic present.

So this mantelpiece and the top of the vast buffet exhibit what's left of passionate loves, explosive divorces and busted *fortunes since the Franco-Prussian war, two Russian Revolutions, two World Wars and, above all, the 1968 revolution where my mother was such a fervent militant urging everybody to "make love, not war," and triggering quite a few private wars in the process. And I am supposed to see a* line *here, finding its apotheosis in the birth of Duncan Godefroy Rabinovitch: ME.*

So here I am, during Spring break, far from Daytona Beach. No parties, no sex! What would my Princeton undergraduate pals think if they knew what I am busying myself with right now? No sex, NO SEX!

Hey, wait a minute, I could imagine something with that girl next to the old general. Real cute, the innocent Bambi profile, the tiny curl that escaped the chaste Biedermeier hat… She is ogling at me. Oh, help me now, smartphone, my only link to the world, to create lasting intimacy! I need a selfie with that girl. Excuse me, general, I have to push you aside. But I must de-frame, free the maiden from her silver prison, divest her from the shame of…being dead. My own cheek will cover one side of the frame, but what to do with the other? Oh yes, that flowerpot over there will do, tiny white flowers will rain over the forbidden part and…click!

"Look at this! I am happy to see you for once

interested in the family." Startled, Duncan knocked over the flowerpot. The failed ballerina had to go on her toes to reach a non-bearded spot on her son's cheek to blow a kiss.

"Interested? I have nothing to do with these old guys."

"Yes, you do. Through *me*!"

"Hmm. Insofar as motherhood cannot be contested like paternity."

"You bastard, get out of here!"

"Oh, I am a bastard? Well, if *you* say so…"

On his way out, absorbed in the picture of his new Biedermeier love interest on his smartphone, Duncan stumbled over the sinuous leg of a Louis XVI chair.

Autsch! Damn all that crooked 'nobility' bought with the blood of thousands of poor cows at a giant Chicago slaughterhouse! Daughters of newly rich butchers, corned beef barons, marrying, nineteen-twenties style, into impoverished European aristocracy. Very sexy. Gosh, this is becoming obsessive. Yes, I do miss sex as such, but perhaps even more so the locker room bragging about it. Not even a ball here!

After roaming around for a while, Duncan continued his musings in the vegetable garden. He gave a hefty kick to a vaguely football-shaped forgotten pumpkin. The rotten pumpkin exploded and slimy seeds clung to Duncan's pant and shoes.

I need a brush, but I am not going back to the house until I am insufferably hungry. Well, I am craving a hotdog which I would not find in that aristocratic refrigerator anyhow. She threw me out, let her worry about my destiny. I'll find a brush in the saddle room next to mom's gelding, that faux Lipizzaner who, presumably was trained by a guy from the Vienna Imperial Riding Academy.

It's nice to be greeted from afar by a neighing and a white horse trotting toward the stable from the paddock, expecting his oats. The old guy seems to like my petting him behind the ears. Should I try to bridle him? Oh, those elaborate bits, must even animals' gear be baroque?

"Here we go, calm, calm, darling, put your head down, please, please, open your mouth, open, open, o-pen! Tha-a-at's it!"

Now the saddle, ornate to fit a sultan. Oh, yes, his name is Sultan, I remember. At least she does not use a ladies' side saddle, although that would be more her style. As to my riding style, the only one I know is Western. She would be horrified if she saw a cowboy on her imperial stallion. I must avoid getting close to the house. I'll try at least to point the tips of my feet in direction of the horse's mouth, not shockingly outward as in the klotzy Western stirrups. My sneakers are too large anyhow for these delicate ones, so no stirrups at all. No spurs either.

Hardly had Duncan swung himself into the saddle that Sultan galloped toward the usually forbidden topiary garden behind the mansion where a certain shrub, tortured into corkscrew shape, was his favourite delicacy.

~ ~ ~

Meanwhile Lucrezia had let her head sink in theatrical despair on her arms folded over the mantelpiece in the library. She lifted it slowly to face the portraits.

*You, my companions since long before my birth, you, my prenatal past, speak to me! I am not given to the present fad of young geeks like Duncan to explore their ancestry in order to find their "true selves" as constituted by their genes in various proportions. A glance at the party assembled on the mantelpiece is proof that that would be a bit difficult in my case and so …*unimaginative!* In contrast, some creative* *genetic manipulation brings you closer to the ideal. More than genes or bloodlines, I crave to perceive the imprint of feelings left by a tumultuous personal and public history. If the face is a mirror of the soul, I must be possible, with some empathy, some feeling-in, to conjure these imprints, make them dimly visible like palimpsests from under the surface traits.*

Other people impose on their visitors a gallery of children, an implicit blackmail to find them sooo cute. Who is interested in other people's children? Well, Duncan, being so exceptionally handsome and deceptively nice, would be decorative here, but nobody alive could match the depth and mystery of the faces so intensely present here.

Reveal yourselves! I find part of my identity in each and every one of you, except in the newest photo, taken in the fifties, that of a dowdy teenager, Gretel, me. No, definitely NOT ME! She is an absolute has-been, gone, DEAD. By the way, that is the only picture of someone still alive, that's why it is so banal. I couldn't see myself as the little girl in Hänsel und Gretel, although I am impregnated by German fairy tales and legends. Oh, all those knights on their white steed, the Siegfrieds, Lohengrins, Parzifals and their damsels in distress! Well, I have never been a damsel in distress and now, at my age, they would not bother saving me. But to have a shining knight like Parzifal as son… I should know better, though. Herzeleyde, Parzifal's mother, Suffering Heart, seems emblematic of mothers. Sorrow over a roaming-around son. Sounds familiar.

Speak to me! Papa, Mutti, you who never refused anything to me, you should be the first to answer my plea. Here you are, side by side in all your vulnerable beauty. I see you floating together, oblivious of reality, over the ruins of a small, bombed-out German town, like Chagall's lovers over the shtetl. On the next picture, even under the Nazi Stahlhelm, *you look so naïve, Papa, so innocent, here facing the young Red Army soldier whom you fought—and perhaps killed—in World War II. Under other circumstances, such as being introduced by ME, you might have become best friends over vodka or our great wine,* Forster Ungeheuer.

Speak to me now, French countess in showers of pearls, my last mother-in-law! You who were so talkative when it came to criticizing me! Don't look so arrogantly down on the innocent maiden in the Biedermeier hat next to you, my great-grandmother. Sorry, no amount of pearls can ever compete with the pearly skin of youth. But…what is all that sand around the girl's picture and the incongruous overthrown flowerpot? Did Duncan hold a memorial ceremony, spreading soil on some beloved one's last resting place? No, that would not be like my pragmatic, insensitive American son. But if it were, he should have chosen my ideal and role model, Anna Pavlova, greatest ballerina of all times and at one time mistress of my last father-in-law, the monocled count near her on the mantelpiece. Her iconic rendering here as the Dying Swan somehow predestined her to be here: the immortal star on, not under a marble plate.

Lucrezia's iconic wide, ballet-length crêpe-de-chine skirt allowed her to execute a deep reverence with *rond de jambe* in front of Pavlova. But she suddenly froze in the movement. Her grandmother, oddly resembling Sitting Bull with her dark, straight black hair parted in the middle and severely pulled back, looked at her disapprovingly from out of her chin-high, black collar.

Mother—or grandmotherly—dissatisfaction has the lasting effect of a cancer that cannot be excised. Oma, you spoilt my elegiac mood!

Furiously, Lucrezia turned the picture around, but now grandma's piercing eyes continued to disapprove from the mirror behind the mantelpiece, like that day when Gretel sneaked out of the house to go to a dance party. Lucrezia slammed the picture flat on its face.

She addressed the Grand Master of Free Masons: *No point in trying to seduce you, pompous Grand Master, I know you would not "yield thine secret knowledge" to an outsider of the Lodge. But my secret knowledge directs me to the small picture hidden by myself behind your big frame: the face and torso of the Russian Adonis, Vladimir, several years younger than I, my love made possible for a very short time by the law of exterritoriality. Oh, Volodia, what could have been if evil forces had not pursued us! For the duration of the divorce procedures, my previous husband had me followed by detectives to prove adultery, which might have showed me as an unworthy mother and given him the guardianship of my beloved, precious child...Duncan! So, my choice of a lover was restricted to diplomats whom I thought I could visit at their place. But I found out that an apartment privately rented by a diplomat was not exterritorial. My choice was, therefore, further narrowed to Soviet diplomats because those lived all together in a compound outside of the city which officially was part of the Soviet Mission to the UN. The divine moment I met you, Volodia, at the photo exhibition of the Ballets Russes at the Library of the Performing Arts where we both happened to stare at Nijinsky as a faun bent over a more than consenting female. We were mesmerized into immobility until I inclined backwards in imitation of the female dancer and you, for all your shyness, could not help taking Nijinsky's position. It was the longest kiss of my life. And you turned out to be a Soviet diplomat!*

Exterritoriality, however, did not protect us for long. After three passionate nights I became a suspect, victim of the ingrained Russian paranoia of "shpion." You were sent back to Moscow, not giving up the belief that Love would always triumph and marriage would erase any bureaucratic blemish. Perhaps. But what kind of a Soviet woman would I have made? Marriage was impossible anyhow because how could Vladimir marry a married woman? For once I was able to see myself as a heroine in the tragedy of star-crossed lovers. I don't know why I still hide your picture, now that there is no jealous husband around anymore. Am I bashful of the intimacy only you ever made me feel? Lucrezia, the faithful woman of one single man? You are the only instance when I was authentically ME.

As to the rest, all is vanity. But wasn't I good at this, this self- parading, small-talking, être branchée? Wasn't I thriving on it? Does my talent fail me today? This company ignores me, I feel snubbed as when, at a cocktail party, your conversation partner keeps looking at the door in case a more interesting person might show up. I used to be able to animate *a party, bring it to life.* LIFE. *Why those petty distinctions? Isn't Marlene or Garbo more alive when seen moving in a film than some live dull Gretel? Men can still fall in love with them, their glamour is an eternal waltz under high above crystal chandeliers. How I am craving for a waltz, preferably in the arms of a glittering uniform…*

Admiral, will you lend me your arm to start the Polonaise?

The admiral's battleship-grey metal frame was pressed against Lucrezia's left breast. *Oh, excuse me one second, Admiral, we need music of course, where is that Polonaise CD? Never mind, the Radetzky march will be fine on the Bose, then the Blue Danube waltz. But we need candles, too, a must for both joyful and, well, funeral festivities. Oh, here are a few in that candle holder, half-burned down, it does not matter, but the matches, not used for so long, don't give any spark. Where did I hide that corpus delicti, my cigarette lighter?*

The only solution is Promethean. I will bring the fire to these mortals, okay, dead mortals from the kitchen. A page torn out from any of these old books can be lit on the gas stove. But the pages are so brittle, they won't form a good torch. Oh, here, Sade is tougher. I am delighted to emasculate him. But to get to the kitchen, I have to cross the hall where I risk bumping into the maid or, worse, that Barbarian son of mine.

Lucrezia put her ear to the library door. No sound on the other side. She ran through the hall, a crumbled Sade in her fist.

While I am in the kitchen, what else do we need for the ball? Oh, I see a bottle of Champagne in the refrigerator because its door was left open. Duncan, of course, that constantly snacking American with no culinary discipline! But, indeed, there must be something to drink at this festivity, there must be, some... libation?

Sure, here is a bottle of Champagne, never mind the name. I'll first bring it to my company, then come back for the flame.

Skirting the façade of the château on the side of the topiary garden in order not to attract anybody's attention by a popping cork, she reached the library where she put the open bottle on the mantelpiece.

Back in the kitchen, she twisted Sade into a torch, carefully brought it back to the library and lit the first candle.

A draft from the open French window caused a flake of red-hot Sade to reach the brittle ancient silk curtains which immediately caught fire.

Lucrezia's scream made a horse in the topiary garden rear and Duncan jumped off. He barely reached the room to pull down the curtains with all his weight and to suffocate the flames which already menaced the dusty velvet backs of the portraits.

He grabbed the picture of his lady fair, put it on a chair to safety and poured the Veuve Cliquot over the departed ones, not before taking a big sip himself. The fire was vanquished.

"My saviour, my hero, my knight!"

"At least you know now that I care for the family."

"And you arrived on a white steed to save your lady fair on that chair, your great-great-grandmother." Lucrezia was still breathless. "And you saved *me*!"

Duncan Godefroy put his arm around her waist.

"Shall we waltz?"

Laetitia's Home

The doctor is good to me. Pays me more than any of my neighbours down in the township receives. He smiles at what he calls my obsession with order. "Do I make so much dirt and disorder, Laetitia? I am rarely here. You could go home so much earlier."

Could go home so much earlier? What for? He doesn't get it.

True, he keeps this apartment just for an occasional late emergency operation at the next-door hospital, but spends most nights up there in Constanza, at his girlfriend's place. The villa looks from outside like one of those…how do they call them?…fortresses?…high on a rock like you see on TV about very old times. Nobody could enter there without special keys and secret numbers and letters, not only through the entrance door, but almost between every stair and room. Outside, roses and blooming shrubs flow down like waves as if they wanted to join the waves of the two oceans that meet far beneath.

I saw it once when bringing up a freshly ironed

dress shirt. It's all so beautiful, but I would be afraid to close myself in by mixing up all those tricks to get from one room to another or push a button that howls. The lady is very beautiful, too, but within all this beauty, I would feel like in a prison if I were in her shoes. Now, if you are in a prison, that means that people don't want you, maybe because they are afraid of you, right? Things are turned upside-down: Mandela was in prison, now the rich white people are, at least I would feel that way.

Somehow, I feel freer down in my shack in the township. But there is too much coming and going, so many people and I cannot keep it clean and neat and orderly, with the dirt floor and the dust coming through the tin roof, although I have patched it here and there with palm branches and banana leaves. They all talk too much, I can never be alone and dream.

In the doctor's apartment, I am the lady of the house for there is no other lady. I am free to put things in the right order, and nobody will disturb that order. On the cupboards in the kitchen, mugs and cups parade in order of size. The forks, knives, and spoons are lodged according to rank: the top drawer houses the silverware with the tiny image scratched on each, something like a tribal shield. Does that mean that the doctor is a chief or nobleman among whites? In the middle drawer I put the ordinary forks and knives, and all the way down is the township of the service crowd, the ladles, meat forks, wooden spoons. The single central drawer above the panzer-like heavy frying pans is the barracks of the kitchen knife warriors. They are on military duty only at rare occasions, when I prepare the doctor's favourite African dish and there are so many fish and vegetables to cut and the kitchen is a battlefield. With their black handles and spear-like blades, they are Zulu warriors, and the smaller ones are their wives and children waiting for them to come home. This is why I must not mix up the compartments.

Up there on the wall, I found the right place for royalty—or is that what Hector, my very educated, always excited neighbour calls the "leisure class"? He probably means someone like the beautiful lady—I call her Constanza, with the copper-colour hair because I only know the name of her place up there. Hector visibly does not like the leisure class, he wants to do away with it and gets specially excited and jumps on the roof of the bicycle shack when he speaks of that fellow called Max or something and his capital. Hector would be angry if he knew that I give the leisure class a place of honour high up on the wall, above the ordinary folks. Why must educated people always be so excited? Well, the doctor is not. He is calm, sure of himself, never angry at anybody or shouting for a change of the order of things. But perhaps that comes from one of the things Hector calls "privilege." The copper pans have no work to do, just to look beautiful and distinguished. So, I placed them high on the white kitchen wall opposite the window so that they reflect the setting sun. At that time, for a few minutes the kitchen is filled with a miracle light, red-gold-purple, a light that could only come from God.

But think of it, I helped God a little bit, didn't I, by hanging the pans up there, by putting things in the right place?

In the broom cabinet, same order of rank, from brooms and mops down to the cleaning rugs hanging to dry on a rope—why do I always think of rank? No, after all, that is not something brought over by the whites. In my Zulu family everybody is more important than everybody else.

Behind the glass doors of the dining room buffet, the crystal forms a Corpus Christi procession, six slim champagne flutes (yes, that's their name) form an honor guard around the Virgin Mary, the most sparkling flower vase. They are followed by all the smaller crowd of the wine and water glasses and the little liquor glass children. I was born on Corpus Christi day and allowed to walk with the procession. My mother had wanted to baptize me "Procession" but uncle Max found this ridiculous and proposed "Lenina." Since nobody knew what to with that name, they pronounced it "Laetitia." On my third birthday I was allowed to follow the procession. I had a little basket with rose petals that I strew along the road. That is my memory of beauty. When the terrace window is open and a soft breeze from the garden blows petals into the room, I pick them up and lay them along the crystal procession.

For my birthday, my sons come from Johannesburg where they both work. They tried to talk me into leaving my place here in the township and coming with them to live in a "real apartment." Once I saw the "real apartment." Yes, it has regularly running water and an easy-to-clean linoleum floor. But…I don't feel it. The doctor's apartment has something like…a glow.

They are good boys, the two of them, they even wanted to send me money every month. I said I don't need the money. They looked at each other with open mouths until finally Charlie said: "It's okay, mom, you are a widow, you can do what you want." I found it amusing, almost flattering, that they take me for a kept girl.

They don't get it.

I bought some gold thread to embroider the round, white dining tablecloth with a sun. Its rays go in all directions from the center where every Sunday I put the Virgin Mary vase filled with marigolds, a small crowd of little suns. It makes me sad that the doctor has not noticed the whole thing, except once when I had not found marigolds at the market and replaced them with much bigger, yellow Chris…something to do with Christ, I suppose, so it was fitting too.

"Oh, the beautiful flowers," he said, "you must have spent a lot of money. I want to reimburse you!"

He doesn't get it.

The last shirt to iron. My favourite one, the one with the blue-and-white narrow stripes which he usually wears with the collar unbuttoned. It goes so well with his blue eyes and his gold- tanned skin I am putting it on a hanger in front of the window to dry out the ironing steam. The air from behind makes it billow, you'd say his breast is filling it.

Even with all the windows open, the air feels so close, seems we are going to have a thunderstorm soon. Or is it the steam from the iron that makes me sweat? I feel like taking a bath. The doctor often told me to take advantage of the "conveniences" of his apartment as he thinks that, down there I am not so well equipped.

Yes, for once I'll do that. I take a bath in his tub. The running lukewarm water makes me strangely dizzy. The image of a short-legged, fiftyish, black woman reflected from all sides by the ceiling-high mirrors, usually witnesses to his naked body, fills me with a long-forgotten shame as I step out of my cheap underwear. I climb into the tub that last contained his body. There is the familiar smell of his shower gel by which I always know, when arriving in the morning, that he spent the night here. I can't close the faucet entirely, the moving water keeps gently flowing, caressing my skin. The fragrant soap that slid over his body slides over mine. It makes the inside of my thighs slippery. I feel…something like…happy.

Love Crucifix

Vivía una joven linda como una flor

…y tu amante quiero ser yo

…voy a morirme de todas muertes

antes de perder mi honor

el mal hermano sacó el revolver… *

*T*he melody of the Mexican Mariachi song remained in my mind. Of the words only those I could fit to the rhythm. Some waltz?

They keep haunting me in my pain.

Having arrived as a young child in Miami with my Cuban parents, working after their death as a room maid at the hotel Château Fontainebleau, at age nineteen I was still a virgin. I was afraid of men after escaping almost daily attempts at rape. All my love and trust belonged to my animal, my brown shepherd mix whom I rescued as a stray dog three years ago.

* *There lived a girl, pretty like a flower/ and your lover I want to be/ I'll die a thousand deaths/ rather than lose my honor/ the villain pulled out his revolver and…*

Then I met the Mexican.

Mexicans are not as numerous here as are Cubans and other Hispanics, I believe. Anyhow, the man seemed different in some inexplicable way.

Granted, with his slender, athletic body he was gorgeous looking, his low-buttoned white shirt and designer's jeans setting off his tan. His eyes, however, were both magnetic and somehow…disquieting. But I told myself that that was my imagination born of painful experience with men.

So, when I met him at the beach on my day off—he happened to enter the water just the moment I did—I accepted his invitation to dinner the following evening at the restaurant of the hotel.

I had just finished cleaning my last room in time to change from my maid's uniform into that pretty blue lace dress a nice lady had given me when I cleared her breakfast tray. She found that I have a more fitting figure than she had now.

I saw him arriving in his silver Porsche convertible—I am not indifferent to such things, my eyes being trained to luxury all day long. He stopped at the main entrance. When I stepped out, the familiar doorman held the door for me with a mockingly deep bow. "Buenas tardes, bella reina, Elena!"

By the time I joined my date to show him the direction to park, three more of my fellow servants were standing open-mouthed next to the doorman.

When we were seated with a view of the ocean, the *MaîtreD* (also one of those...), while putting my lobster cocktail in front of me, slid his left finger over the nude part of my back, out of sight of my companion. Standing behind my partner, the wine steward who filled his Champagne flute gave me a wink. Then he filled up mine again. I had emptied my first one fast to overcome some discomfort, probably my shyness.

Now I felt more confident, perhaps too confident. Although I know it is bad manners to ask a new acquaintance immediately what he does for a living as if you were testing his financial and social status, my curiosity got the better of me. "I'm in horses, well, and dogs," he replied with a short laugh. Why that laugh?

The idea of being with someone whose calling was the care of my favorite animals—I am volunteering at Miami's equestrian center and they let me ride for free

—made me respond to the slight pressure of his hand on mine. What a gentleman he was. Would anybody else have been so eager to learn about my preferences on a menu? Anyhow, I did not know what most of the names of the dishes meant. He suggested, I accepted.

He also suggested we meet again. I accepted. After dinner, we took a short stroll along the beach. He did not make any of those moves I expect and fear from experience. I said I had to go home because my parents insisted that I be back before midnight. That was a lie. I live in a small cottage next to the hotel sharing it with another room maid. But the lie had helped sometimes.

"Of course, I understand," he said. "Cuban parents have a reputation of being strict."

Nobody had ever kissed my hand—and only my hand—when saying good-bye.

The next day I wanted to be beautiful—that desire was nothing new as such but this time I wanted a particular man to desire me and this new feeling made me slightly apprehensive.

Was I still in control of myself? Why did I put on these stiletto heels so inappropriate for an excursion to the country?

The Porsche was already waiting for me at the parking. Not used to such low-built sports cars, I entered clumsily and my left stiletto slashed the passenger seat's leather upholstery by a long tear.

I was so embarrassed that I started to cry. Not even checking out the damage, he pulled me into the seat and put his arms around me.

"Don't cry, my beloved, this is nothing, so easily repaired, don't cry, I beg you, it's nothing!"

He leaned over from the driver's seat to kiss my tears away and his lips slid down to my mouth. For the first time I felt a violent desire to belong.

He did not exploit my state of mind which he must have guessed, feeling my body melt under his embrace. He sat up again in his seat.

"Let's go to the horses, they will make you forget that mishap which isn't one."

After some half-hour drive away from the city toward the open countryside, there appeared from afar a vast hill of luminous green, spotted by mighty elms, surrounded by white-painted wooden fences responding to the white of the large bungalow at the center. Three gorgeous thoroughbreds came galloping as we approached the gate.

I had hardly the time to admire the interior of the house when a servant announced that a business partner needed to see him outside. He jumped up.

"I'll be right back, dearest," he excused himself and ordered the servant to bring me a drink, his personal Tequila cocktail "only a Mexican could create" before dashing outside through the back entrance.

After a few minutes and a sip from the indeed delicious cocktail, I don't know what curiosity prompted me to step out by the French door he had taken no time to close and to approach the distant back of the property which was hidden by a high and dense row of flowering laurel trees.

I walked toward a hardly visible opening in the laurel row. On the other side, after a bend of the dusty dirt path ending in a field framed by sickly trees, there were rusty barbed-wire enclosures where other horses were crammed together with mules, donkeys and goats, all looking starved or wounded, some with burn marks, some maimed.

My heart stopped. For I don't know how long, I

could not move, my fingers cramped on the barbed wire.

Suddenly he stood close behind me.

"Why did you come here? I told you I would be back in a moment!"

Through a knot in my throat I managed to ask: "Are…these…rescue animals?"

"They are. They would be dead if we had not brought them here. We take care of them."

He put his arm around my shoulder. "Let's go back to the house, it's getting windy."

Indeed, the wind had turned, and now the howling and wailing of dogs, intermittently interrupted by drums, could be heard from afar. Lightning struck my Cuban brain: El toque de santo…santería…religious sacrifice…voodoo!

In vain I tried to free myself from his embrace. "You will be mine!"

He tore open my blouse. "Stop the comedy, you are nothing but one of the hotel whores, why are you making it difficult for me?"

Just at that moment, a Range Rover arrived from the other side of the grounds. He had to let go of me.

Throwing away my stiletto shoes, I ran out of sight through a patch of thorny bushes. My skirt was torn, I pulled out a piece of it to cover my exposed breast, all the while running with bleeding feet across the shrubs in search of a road, any road, where I might find a bus stop. I finally reached a small road, but no bus stop in sight. No passing car either. And if there had been one with a single male driver, I would not have dared to stop it anyhow. Suddenly there was a silver Porsche dashing by. That direction had to be avoided then, but I did not know where I was.

Of how I got home the police report could give you a more precise image. Somebody, it seems, had found me sitting, exhausted and intoxicated by some Mexican drug sometimes added to Tequila, at the side of the little road.

All this is of no importance, nothing is of importance to me anymore. There was silence when I got back to the cottage, not the usual excited greeting bark of my beloved Amorcito.

After my roommate Alicia had overcome her shock over my appearance, she announced that a large package had arrived for me—not by postal service but hand-delivered by a man.

"Shall I bring it to you?" she asked. "It's heavy."

I was still too stunned to wonder who could have sent me a big package. I have no parents, no siblings, no…lover.

There was only one, Amorcito—and he was not there.

Alicia startled, I must have cried out in pain when she dragged the package into the room.

The thick cardboard was held together by a raw, dirty rope, its almost triangular form resembling an ancient coffin. Certain spots of the cardboard were softened by blood seeping through. I threw myself to the floor, tore the strings open with my teeth and I ripped the cardboard apart.

He was inside, Amorcito.

His paws cut off, his belly opened lengthwise, covered with half-dried blood. His ears had been synched, one eye burnt out, the other hanging out on a thread. The paws must have been severed first for, at the stumps the blood was brown and dry while on breast and head there was fresh, red blood.

The torture must have gone on for hours.

His jaws broken apart, holding between them a stick to form a Christian cross with the elongated body.

"Get this horror out of the room," Alicia shrieked.

I could only throw myself on the corpse to press my lips on the single not blood-covered spot, the soft brown fur between what had been the eyes that I had so often kissed. I needed to protect him one last time.

I was not murdered like the girl in the Mexican song.

My companion was.

So was, in front of the crucifix, Love within me— forever.

The Project

Yet another screech from my spade protesting to be pushed against a stone. This unyielding earth, full of flint and run-through by ancient roots! Will I be able to go ahead with the burial of those who were my children some sixty years ago?

I have to make a pause to stretch. The sky on this October afternoon looks so morning-like, so spring-like, radiating with summer pleasures to come.

For me?

Will I still see another summer and if so, how much will my dimming eyes see of it? Will I still be able to bend down to caress my dog?

What is certain is that the companions of my childhood must not be desecrated after my death. They would be thrown into that big garbage can over there. To save them from such an end must be my project here and now.

For the ritual, it would be much easier to build a pyre, simply by piling up a few of the fallen oak and beech branches further up in the park.

But it is unthinkable to throw the beloved stuffed animals of my childhood into the flames.

The German Steiff creatures followed me to all my successive residences—which were as numerous as the men in my life—ending up in the last one, this crumbling château in France. Their "hides" became threadbare, moth-eaten here and there, but they maintained their graceful form and the touching expression of their faces.

The muzzle of the teddy bear, the foal, the deer are bare of their original velvet for having been kissed too often by the lonely child who preferred their company to that of the neighbour children in the courtyard, who animated the animals, giving each of them a soul.

They are the forebears of all the live animals of my later years who carried their names, the horse, cats, dogs, rabbits and the almost tame wild birds which came visiting my windowsill.

There is continuity—or do I tend to be more sensitive to representation, art, artefact than to reality? Reality is always escaping into various presentations by different people.

The stability of anonymous representation made me feel safe. The key to reality was missing all my life, but I was not trying too hard to find it, preferring my dreamy cocoon.

Helga's had been a dreamy fairy tale marriage. With her French count, the shy, provincial, romance-reading girl had entered aristocracy as prescribed by fairy tales and romance literature.

Meanwhile cosmopolitan aristocracy had become part of the jet set, and many of her conventional, petty-bourgeois assumptions were challenged. Yet she continued to cling to the sentimental, romantic aura projected by her mother that illuminated her childhood.

The tomb must be profound enough not to be touched by the gardener's spade once I am gone. Only if the mansion is torn and bulldozers prepare the grounds for, say, a commercial district and parking lot, will the remains of the animals be destroyed.

But the permit to do that will demand such lengthy legal battles between conservationists and developers that my beloved ones will have time to integrate the dark earth under generations of autumn leaves.

Let's give the spade another push, too bad for the arthritis in my elbows.

"Qu'est-ce que vous faites là, Madame la Comtesse ? »

Rigaud, a man from the neighbouring village, was suddenly standing next to her.

How long had he been observing her, always eager

for some non-tax-declared odd job?

I hate this peasant habit of dropping in. Nobody in Paris would visit unannounced. I have no answer ready about what I am doing here, no should I have to give one—to someone so representative of the local xenophobia (even a Parisian is a stranger) in constant inner conflict with their greed.

"Oh, rien de spécial, Monsieur Rigaud…I just had this idea…"

"Do you want me to bring my digging machine? You won't be able to make a hole here by hand. Not even me. And I am younger and stronger than you."

Thanks for the reminder, tactless oaf.

Is stressing your physical superiority intended to make me feel helpless, hence more inclined to pay for services?

"No, thanks. For the moment I don't need anything, Monsieur Rigaud."

Now he has noticed the blanket on which the animals are neatly laid to provisional rest. He looks at me, scrutinizing, asking himself how long it will take for me to be institutionalized. Indeed, he surprised me last week when I was rummaging upstairs to retrieve the toy animals—he saw the mad woman in the attic. Now he must be figuring out what would be in for him in my progressive dementia. Most likely he will be the first to notice and later declare it, giving himself all the time to take a look at my drawers before. He wouldn't find much there, and he does not understand a thing about antiques.

Only once he admired an object: the kitschy Japanese souvenir shop figurine, gift of a former maid, which I did not throw out, because I liked the hunch-backed old woman, and she may notice its absence at one of her visits with her gift of fresh eggs. He has neither key nor code to the safe.

He does not move, apart from his eyes which are now busy to fix the exact location of my attempted hole: so many yards diagonally from the oak, so many laterally from the beech, straight from the kitchen window—just in case I intend to bury a treasure here. He would be the only one to know. The irony: what is so much more than a material treasure to me would turn out to be a dire disappointment to him. His metal detector might signal something to him, but it could only be the tiny bell on the toy cow's neck.

Pretending to straighten my back, I lift my head above the stocky, low-class intruder.

"I don't need anything today, Monsieur Rigaud," I repeat, stressing the "Monsieur." *This must be a remnant of my youthful egalitarian idealism: why, among two persons, should one be given name, title and, in Latin languages, the respectful second person plural, while the other is merely called by his first name? At the same time, the acquired aristocratic part of my existence taught me the necessity of class distinctions. Stay formal. Those people take the slightest gesture of familiarity as an entitlement. If I called him Roland, he'd call me Helga. Unacceptable.*

"Bon, alors bonsoir, Madame la Comtesse."

I never asked to be called by my title. But they are either slyly deferent of outright insolent. Formerly small farmers, most of them are now factory workers at a car manufacturing plant, they were brainwashed by their union bosses brandishing Marx and Trotsky whom, of course, they never read to justify their greed for private property. Now he is walking away stiffly, I bet he is counting the steps between my cache and the service entrance to the property.

Suddenly the dog started yelping, running back and forth between the "grave site" and the back door. The telephone must be ringing. With an agility surprising for her age, ran to the back entrance of the house.

Would she ever lose the teenage excitement at the ring of the phone? An invitation to a party, a ball? A suitor calling?

Indeed, apart from Rigaud, the only living person

she had spoken with during the last forty-eight hours was the car repair man.

Would it for once be someone caring, someone who'd ask about the animals or how she was spending her day? The latter question would be embarrassing. Telling about the project of the burial? Only to a child could the child of yore talk about it without being ridiculous.

She unhooked the receiver from the rectangular rotary phone on the wall. It was the president of the local stag hunting club.

"Bonjour, Madame la Comtesse, please allow me in the name of our members to repeat our invitation to join the club."

"*Me?* Join *your* club!"

"Madam, you don't have to be a huntress to join but you would enjoy get-togethers in our private homes, our concerts of sonneurs de cor (horn players , vins d'honneur and so on. After all, you belong to our milieu, to the noble tradition of the Saint Hubert."

The noble tradition! It took Helga a moment to react.

How dare he to call me, the guy whose horse refused to jump my fence beyond which the young stag, already wounded by the hounds, had sought refuge. The master of the hunt lay on the ground, one foot still hanging in the stirrup, his face hurt by his own spur. My enjoyment of the scene disappeared as soon as I stood next to the animal collapsed on the grass. It was obvious he was beyond saving. Anyhow, what veterinarian would have dared to intervene in the noble tradition of chasse à courre?

Contrary to me, the master's companions showed themselves humane and dismounted to help him get up. While doing so, they visibly fought to grab the knife for the honor of "finishing-up the animal."

The honorable tradition! And to think that I myself took part in this! Out of snobbism or the primitive excitement shared with the horses and hounds, the smell of autumnal forests, the champagne "coup de l'étrier" before mounting? Insensitive moron I was! True, I hated the halali and discontinued my participation after a couple of seasons. Now I hate them all, those self-infatuated idiots proudly posing next to the exposed bowels of the "defeated" animal.

Helga did not know whom she hated more, the hunters or her former self which fueled her furor, searching for the most humiliating insult to a horseman, the reminder of his failure to control his mount.

"Your horse is smarter than you, he understood the illegality of trespassing private territory and he refused to jump."

"Illegality? Not exactly, Madame la Comtesse. It is a tradition of courtesy on the part of landowners to make their grounds available to Saint Hubert hunters when the pursued animal enters them."

Helga dropped the receiver letting it dangle from its cord

What they really want is not me but the permission to invade my land for the fun of killing. I hear steps on the gravel outside. I feel like pulling that rusty sword from its sheath there in the corner before going back outside to see who is coming.

"Emilie!"

The seven-year-old was becoming more graceful by the day. Framed by the still open backdoor and lit from behind by the setting sun, the slim silhouette with only the blond hair illuminated was a child fairy apparition.

"Je suis venue te donner une bise," Emilie announced, stretching to reach Helga's cheek to place a kiss.

"And to sit on the horse," Helga said with a wink. "But I am not sure if Aicha is in the mood to be saddled. She is becoming a grouchy old lady, you know."

"No, Aicha is not grouchy. My dad says that you are a grouchy old lady and you are not."

"Not with you."

"Can you at least lift me up so I can pet Aicha behind the ears, she loves that. Then I can brush her and walk her around with Wolfie," she added, having just spotted the dog outside.

Following him with her eyes, she discovered the blanket with the stuffed animals.

"Oh, you brought them out! They haven't been on the grass for a long time, they will be happy. Can we both play with them?"

"Play?"

"Sure, give them a birthday party like the other day for Foxie. I bring out the plates and cups and make a cake with carrots and oats. We also invite Aicha and Wolfie and Eh-Ah and, well, just me and you like last time."

"So, you want a party?"

"A party, sure! Whose birthday is it today?"

"You decide. You still do have power over time."

"What do I have?"

"You want to celebrate a new year in somebody's life. I was planning another kind of celebration: a funeral."

"You mean like for dead people?"

"In a way, yes," Helga said hesitatingly. "You mean they are alive?"

"Well, they have always been…after all, you and I made birthdays for them, so…"

Helga put her arm around Emily's shoulder, avoiding looking at her face. "I thought they would be better off in the living earth than in the dusty, dead attic. Come help me!"

The sadness Helga feared to see on Emily's face did not appear. She was all eagerness at the new task. With astounding strength, the flower elf pushed the spade into the burial site but gave up over a strong root.

"The spade is no good. I'll get something better."

She ran into the house and came back dragging the vacuum cleaner. "We'll just suck out all the dirt."

The non-plugged vacuum cleaner did not work.

"Anyhow," Helga tried to console her, "that would not work for the stones and the roots of the trees."

"And wouldn't the trees cry if we hurt their roots? We must look for a better place."

"You are right, the trees might cry. Their roots are their lifeline. But what other place?"

"I know! The riding rink. The sand there is so soft that you let me make sand cookies from it, but they crumbled."

"Yes, that is a processed sand brought here from the beach because it is soft to the horses' hoofs and keeps them from slipping. The soil here is loamy, it becomes slippery when wet and hard like clay when the sun bakes it. Remember your cookies that turned to stone?"

"So what? We did not want to eat them anyhow. We'll dig in the corner of the riding rink where Aicha never steps. You always chided her for cutting the corners."

Dig she did, after fetching a ladle from the kitchen as the spade proved too long for her to manoeuvre.

"Wolfie, will you stop digging holes into the lawn, bad boy!" Helga yelled from the rink.

"There must be an animal living there, a mole perhaps," Emily speculated.

"Yes, there is life beneath the earth and perhaps beyond," Helga muttered rather to herself.

With her ladle, the girl had dug out the grave in no time. Now she dragged the stuffed animals—which included a mole—in a bundle made with the blanket. She also brought an antique music box from the attic for ceremonial sounds that happened to play a French Cancan.

Together they lowered the departed and covered the tomb with the sand from the sea and a few late blooming Asters.

Tears showed in Helga's eyes.

None in Emilie's.

"Ah, she is bothering you again, Madame la Comtesse!"

Rigaud shook his daughter by the shoulders.

"You know you are not allowed to come here by yourself, bothering Madame! Your mother is very angry. She'll give you a spanking, she is in such a mood."

Now tears did fill Emily's eyes.

"Emily does not bother me at all, Monsieur Rigaud! She is welcome," Helga screamed but instantly controlled herself in order to buy time.

"Oh, Monsieur Rigaud, I forgot, there is a leak in the yellow guest bathroom. I'll show you. While you take a look, Emily can stay and finish what she is doing."

"Sure, Madame la Comtesse. Let me get the tools from the basement."

Rigaud took his time, stretching a ten-minute plumber's job to an hour's pay while Helga was looking pensively at the early dusk from an upstairs window.

She saw Emily crossing the big lawn, pushing a wheelbarrow, the dog at her side.

"Wolfie has dug them out," the girl confessed.

I will never know whether Emily lied for the good cause of saving the animals or whether there was a genuine complicity between the child and the animal.

That child should have a future.

With this family, she won't have any.

Her mother's face still bears traces of former beauty while, at not yet thirty, it is spongy, swollen and marked by purple

Calvados liquor lines. Will Emily resemble her in fifteen years? Will all the grace be crushed under these people's heavy boots?

She must get out of here.

She must receive an education.

Here I feel I might be able to do something. It will be a double expense, to be sure, for in addition to pay for her studies in Paris, I will have to compensate the family for missed income.

In this part of the country, most children are expected to be wage earners from age fourteen on, right after the mandatory school years. And, as long as they live at home, to compensate the parents for bed and board.

Given the unemployment rate in this region, the parents will easily accept my offer.

Nobody shares my love for this crumbling, humid mansion. After my death, everything I still have value for would be thrown into the dumpster. Except, of course, the paintings, furniture and carpets of monetary value.

And if the sale—and possible demolition—of this old mansion and any proceeds from the saved heirlooms could serve a different kind of conservation, not everything would be senseless anymore.

I would have a project. I would have power over time.

The following Capriccio was first published in French in the journal Passages, *Paris.*

Cancer Fashionista

$\mathscr{A}$ needle stuck in my left wrist, slightly scratching the bone. It was the sting of a transparent tube by which I was suspended to some sort of gallows. At the horizontal bar of the gallows, a plastic bag was attached. From there, through the tube, drops of a poison cocktail descended one by one into my blood.

"Would you like to play some music?"

An exaggeratedly smiling feel-good volunteer handed me a mini-xylophone and a cotton-wrapped tiny hammer to tap on it.

"Let's play Jingle Bells!"

"N-no…thanks…perhaps later…"

Five minutes later, another radiant face solicited my creativity:

"Would you like to do some painting? Just complete this drawing here, then you can colour it…"

Five minutes later, as the poison started to make me feel like throwing up, a triumphantly healthy face, resembling a model from a Snapple advertising campaign suggested some ice cream.

"No? A Snicker? A soda? No? A cookie?"

As I kept staring at the tube, one after one of the well-intended passed to the next patient whose grey-greenish complexion made the apple faces seem a provocation.

To tear myself away from the Medusa effect of the slow descent of the drops, my right hand scribbled on the back of the *Cancer Patient Feel Good* instructions in search of…what?

A memoir? A memento mori? A revelation of the purpose of it all? Not much like me, though, who, in spite of haughty intellectual pretentions, had to fight all my life against the tendency to follow just any hype— fashion-dictated, dietary, academic, ideological…an uphill battle. My physical appearance was of no help. For instance, I avidly seized the new opportunity to stroll topless, which was allowed on the beaches of St. Tropez, encouraged to do so by my then husband who enjoyed showing off proprietorship.

Quite a few years later, one husband substituted by another, Paris substituted by New York, a doctorate earned in the then fashionable semiotics, I felt the trendy need to reinvent myself (yes, like Madonna, including cabbala). And then came the revelation, the apocalypse: I was diagnosed with breast cancer.

No one could fail to notice the recent breast cancer mania, especially exalted by the media. There is an avalanche of reports with tear- provoking photographs of the heroically smiling victim surrounded by her children dipping eyes or noses with Kleenex. Husbands appear more rarely and if they do, look more uncomfortable than tragic. But even the cat, species supposedly indifferent to human suffering, consoles the patient by curling up on her lap.

We learn by the legend that the teenage son has finally removed the piercings from his nose and lips and the daughter promised less concentration on her smartphone and more on her studies, all this to alleviate their mother's tragic fate. The reader is seized by Fear and Pity but reassured by the *deus ex machina* in the person of the devoted doctor who refuses resignation. Group picture of patient, children, cat, and doctor.

She knows she has only a couple of years to live, but those years will be full of meaning. She has now a clear view of her priorities. She has found herself.

Other examples of feel-good are a poetry project, "Prickly Pear," creativity as therapy, especially for the bereaved ones left behind. The eulogies report the battle against the Archenemy (cancer forms together with Al Qaeda and AIDS a Trinity of successors to the medieval devil), accompanied by heart-rending confessions of the survivor: during their last years together, the newly departed had prodigiously gotten on the nerves of his partner who understood only at the moment of death how much he had loved him deep inside.

And the charities, most of them thinly disguised commercial intentions! Their ads obliterate regularly my tool bar.

"Today's cause: fight breast cancer, let's be warriors in pink! Donate!"

"Buy the brand Pink to support the Foundation for Cancer Research. Donate!"

"Do your jogging in a pink T- shirt in sign of solidarity. Order your size now!"

At the other end of the spectrum, you find the good mood of the cancer business: publicity for hospitals where you will be happily pampered, self-help books, women's art, videos, apps, and all the sources of personal self-renewal, such as gyms, spas, cancer yoga, salons for personalized wig creation, lingerie. Victoria's Secret responded to a mass petition for sexy cancer bras. All is but a question of the right attitude, "think pink," which implies your readiness to "invest in yourself," read: spend a lot of money on yourself for somebody else's profit. Breast cancer becomes cool, the hottest subject of the media.

The Nuclear Test Site.

The mercy of a nurse unhooked me from the gallows. I slumped into a deep chair in the recovery room of St. Luke's-Roosevelt hospital after this further torture following the biopsy that revealed the tumour.

Needles, my phobia since childhood! My mother, so skilled in needlework and, by WWII necessity, mending socks with the help of a wooden "sock egg," was desperate about my refusal to learn "that noble art sung by the poets." Yeah, Helen of Troy, high up at a window of her palace, embroidering fine linen with the deathly scenes of the battle raging about her down at the walls. A far cry from mother's yarn and darn and the sock egg.

Mama, most warm-hearted of mothers, became tyrannical when household virtues were the issue. Ah, those generations of young girls who spoiled their eyes by embroidering their initials white on white in relief on sheets, pillowcases, and napkins, all in preparation for some hypothetical husband.

Interesting: the Webster derives the word "hype" from "hypodermic needle." Etymologically dubious it seems, but semantically plausible. This association with a needle should by itself prevent me from ever falling prey to a hype or addiction. Yet, in my present state, how much would I have welcomed a high, such as described by heroin users! Instead, as a punishment for my ancient refusal to pass a thread through the eye of a needle, my right breast had been transformed into a needle cushion, something reminiscent of Kafka's punishing machine. I must have grimaced.

"Are you in pain?"

A hand put itself softly on my wrist.

"Yes…no…not really. I was just thinking of needles and of the risk to be…how do you say 'emasculated' for a woman? De-feminized? Breasts cut off, hair falling out…?"

"Fear of losing your sex-appeal? But, as you read in all the brochures they distribute here, this is our chance at renewal. To start with, calm your nerves by acupuncture."

"Needles! Again!"

"No, renewal! Look: for the time being, I still resemble the old Cassandra Smith, but you will see. And this is Rivka Spielvogel, we met last week during our…magic…radiant…imagination, no, magnetic resonance imagining or something, MRI."

"Pleased to meet you, Cassandra, Rivka. I am Christine."

We shook hands. A "support group" had spontaneously formed.

From that moment on, we behaved as though on the stage of an off-off Broadway comedy.

The exchange covered virtually all the present hypes, except weight loss, as chemotherapy spoils the appetite anyhow.

RIVKA: "You have such a sweet accent, Christine. Are you French?"

CHRISTINE: "No, I was born German but invented myself as French when marrying my first husband. And as Spanish when falling in love with a Flamenco dancer."

CASSANDRA: "Your French revolution, I mean, reinvention, couldn't be more authentic. This elegance, this allure!"

I felt nothing less than elegant in my sneakers. My self-esteem is in direct proportion to the number of inches of my heels. But I know the American admiring prejudice toward all things French—except the pretention of being a world power.

Paris, oh là,là, from fashion to cheese to l'Amour, from Chanel no. 5 to deconstructionist philosophy …"

CA: "Look, here we are, three females slightly over fifty. We do not belong to the texting generation of millennials, nor do we 'hang out' and 'hook up.' We have to be more sophisticated, that's the challenge. We must be artists. And the essence of art is to create illusions.

R.: "Let's do drag, then."

CH.: "But transvestites don't even try to create credible illusions. They invite us to play on the temporary suspension of "normal" judgment, on the glitter of all the facets of desire. As to transgender…"

CA.: "That is a radical choice. We are not here by choice. Besides, if we were men, we would defiantly expose our non-fascist skinheads, pretending that this is our style, a choice of our free will."

CH.: "Ah, if the "right attitude" were all you need! I try to 'think positive,' 'accept myself,' and yet, even with my bald head, cannot resist the hair accessories glanced at in the supermarket, those faux mother-of-pearl hair slides…"

CA.: "By all means, buy those mother-of-pearl hair slides and decorate your wig with them. Who cares for authenticity, what counts is the visual effect. And don't forget those flattering Fedoras and pick-a-boo bangs attached. But most important, the wig."

R.: "But that's a prosthesis! Freud says that prostheses are uncanny, of a disquieting strangeness, because of the uncertainty between live or dead, organic or mechanic."

CA.: "Good old Freud, may he rest in peace. In our era, if our brains can be substituted by artificial intelligence and we are progressively becoming cyborgs, a mere replacement of our skull's cover is certainly less uncanny."

R.: "I myself experienced the wig as uncanny when I was going to be married, and my mother-in-law to be forced me to shave my head and to wear a wig."

CH. (sliding her fingers through Rivka's splendid red-golden mane): "But this is not a wig, or is it?"

CA.: "You see? You cannot even distinguish the fake from the authentic!"

CH.: "I can now when feeling, not only seeing it. So, your hair grew back—by permission of your mother-in-law? You must have reinvented yourself from submissive daughter-in-law-to…"

R.: "…to pain-in-the-neck. That's what she says."

CH.: "What about your husband?"

R.: "Moishe? Like every husband, he plays ostrich when witnessing squabbles between his mother and his wife. Anyhow, he is too busy: when he is not haggling diamonds, he prays."

CA.: "Now, Rivka, why do you call a wig a

prosthesis, which suggests uncanny, metallic mechanisms clicking. Think of it rather as a soft hat, a fur hat..."

CH.: "Fur! I'd rather go naked than wearing fur!"

R.: "Oh, me too, I am a member of PeTA, I manifested in front of Fendi and Bloomingdale's in my former sapphire mink coat which I had spray-painted blood-red. Fur is murder. By the way, in our position as patients, we must refuse any treatment extracted from or tested on animals. I am a lawyer. I demand transparency. The consumer has a right to know what he ingests."

CA.: "Must you Jews and Germans always ruminate ethical issues? That usually leads to fights. But if you absolutely need philosophical depth, keep in mind that aesthetics are deeper than skin-deep. If you find a look that matches your interior being, your invented virtual self acquires a degree of reality that does not have to be immutable..."

R.: "Oh, Cassandra, have mercy on us!"

CA.: "Try to understand! When I was the most obnoxious teenager on our block on Frederick Douglass Boulevard, my parents, good, old-fashioned

Baptists, prayed to God that I might 'find myself.' I did not find myself and I am not sure I want to congeal into a definite, single identity. It is so exciting to explore possibilities. The good news is…"

CH.: "The good news! You are such an optimist, Cassandra."

CA.: "Thanks for the reference. I know my first name does not fit. About that, I found myself in a protracted war with my parents. Mind you, I hold an MA in classics, specializing in Homer. So I always wonder what got into the heads of African Americans of that period when they gave their children the names found in the works of those very 'white, male, dead authors' they wanted at any price to be removed from college syllabi: all these Medeas, Andromedas, Clytemnestras…In my class, there was an Ishtar from Babylon, Long Island, New York, that is. Among my student friends at Columbia, there was a Penelope from Ithaca, NY. Many of the girls reinvented themselves later as Africans—mostly of Nigerian Ibo or Igbo inspiration, or manifested their independence of mind by non-conformist spellings like Mariah or Condoleezza that make any linguist cringe. But back to headgear, most insurances pay for wigs if needed for attested psychological reasons. No all of them, though, you have to google."

R.: "Not all of them? What about the legislators, the government? Discrimination! If Iraq or Afghanistan veterans are treated free for post-traumatic stress symptom, cannot we, victims of the most traumatizing fight, petition our elementary right to equal treatment, not only physical but psychological, like a mind-lifting wig to save us from depression?"

CA.: "And what is more elementary than an accessory?"

R.: "As a tort suit lawyer fighting for compensation of those who were harmed, I am thinking of a class suit. We are powerful because we are legion."

CA.: "Hey, that's good news! Go, go, Rivka! But wait a minute…who is the defendant?"

R.: "That is a problem of strategy. I'd say the usual suspects: legislative, executive, judicial. Or corporations with deep pockets, so far my preferred adversaries because they are more amenable to settlement, be it only to shake off a wasp like me."

CA.: "I love the wasp, it sounds so Socratic. So,

what you do, you harass them by invoking the inequality of revenues…"

R.: "Yes, between those of the obese cleaning woman and the CEO of the company that manufactures vanilla ice cream without clearly indicating on the box that it contains sugar and cream. To take it for granted that everybody understands 'sucrose' as ingredient, that is elitist at best, fraudulent at worst by deliberately hiding a truth that would keep consumers away. Basically, the majority of cases that I represent as a tort suit contingency lawyer—paid only if I win and therefore accepting only those cases that I am sure to win—are of the banana peel accident variety."

CA.: "Rivka, we must pool our resources. I am in Public Relations/Marketing. Until now I was useful only to those companies which you attack. I owe my moment of glory to a brand of cookies I led to victory by convincing the public that, far from causing obesity, those cookies favour a healthy metabolism, especially as they contain omega three, or whatever was the hype of the moment, I don't remember."

CH.: "Aha! Don't you by any chance do publicity

for all the apps of post-cancer renewal?"

CA.: Hey, that would be an idea, I'll sure think of it. As to your idea, Rivka, we will have to officialize our enterprise as a non-profit association, the Association of Victims of Breast Cancer (ABCV), no, not victims but – oh, darn, here again the phallo-centrism—what is the feminine form of 'victor'? We need visibility. I'll ask you to work on the legal bases for some radio, magazine, TV spots. We are fighting against discrimination of women in general and of cancer- challenged women in particular."

CH.: "Couldn't we be a bit more focused?"

R.: "Leave it to me, I'll find some mediatic culprits. And here I have a job for you, Christine, as you speak Spanish since your flamenco affair. One learns a language in no time while dancing with a Latin lover, right?"

CH. (clicking her fingers castanet-like, tapping her non-existing heels on the linoleum floor): "He is the best educational institution."

R.: "I need you because my typical client is a Hispanic lady who knows another Hispanic lady whose cousin just won a million-dollar suit for having slipped on a banana peel or stumbled on a defective step at the entrance to some conspicuously rich building. That's why I often regret not to speak the language of my most promising clients. Racist offenses are even more lucrative, and there I may plead even more convincingly because I feel it."

CA.: "You feel it as a Jew? I scoff them off with a shrug. What I find offensive is Affirmative Action. It is offensive because condescending."

CH.: "You are elitist within your own race."

R.: "Let's not quarrel. We must be united because united we will win. Politicians and corporations cannot ignore our cause without losing their reputation and facing related suits, for well-publicized lawsuits spawn more lawsuits. The amount earned through fundraising and the threat of suits will be the seed money for our own investments, as we become shareholders of the very firms we attack and; therefore, vote in their general assemblies. Take my word for it, nothing scares more the members of the board than a bunch of anti-capitalists among their shareholders, especially of the feminist, ecologist, and animal rights variety. We will be non-profit, of course, which gives us moral superiority over the plutocrats. Our funds constitute a war chest."

CA.: "You'll have to find a legal legerdemain to prevent me from falling into a conflict of interest situation."

R.: "Indeed, since you work with the exploiters, you can be a precious mole. I'll tell you as we go what insider information we need. Don't worry, even if someone of the top guys dares to have suspicions about you, you certainly have him under control thanks to the powerful hashtag 'me too,' With your figure, you surely have been molested."

CA.: "I try to remember such an incident. When I started out, we were not yet made so susceptible. I must have grown a mental armour blocking out such issues for the sake of my career. Anyhow…(she lifts a paper cup from the water cooler) let's drink to the birth of ABCV (Association of Breast Cancer Victims), the trium..trium…darn, again, what is the feminine equivalent of triumvirate, the reign of three men?"

R.: "You see, yet another example of male exclusivity. Hand two more cups and let's celebrate the birth of AVBC, even with the lukewarm water of this water cooler! Stand up, raise your right hand to swear allegiance to AVBC. We should have a hymn. ABC could stand for musical notes, but V? "

CA.: "Variations on ABC. ABC in itself, the first three notes on the octave, would be a rather dull tune. Variations on it should turn it into an incendiary march. You are right, music is as important as format and strategy. We must also link our campaign to official dates, graft AVBC on established causes. If there is a Gay Pride parade, here could be a Cancer Pride parade. February 4 has been declared International Cancer Day. But that sounds like a plea for pity. I want to express the pride. I have a disc jockey friend who mixes rap, Gregorian plain chant and military marches. So what are we waiting for?"

CH.: "Fabulous! If there is reinvention, it might as well be radical. What wig will you wear for the march?"

CA.: "After ample reflexion, I would be a black peroxide Marilyn. But I have to tone down my decibels in order imitate Monroe's simpering baby voice."

CH.: "Dress in pink. That used to be the colour of

baby girls. Now it fits cancer girls."

CA.: "The good news is that wigs have bangs which hide the tiny growth around the face. I would not have Michelle Obama's problem with the frizzle peeking out from under hair so strongly stiffened that it makes you think of a low-roofed Swiss chalet. And what would be your choice for the parade?"

R.: "No wig. I'll go as skin head to protest anti-Semitism."

CH.: "To protest against it by adopting the neo-Nazi symbol? What is the logic?"

R.: "A homeopathic logic. That would destroy the macho menace and let subsist only the pitiful ridicule."

CA. "That won't work. In order to be understood you would have to tattoo swastikas on your bald head and other strategically important parts of your body. And even that would be without effect in a parade because too small to be visible at distance."

CH.: "Then walk between two explanatory cardboards like a sandwich man?"

CA.: "No Way! If one has to explain a suggestive image, it's a flop. Like a joke, it has to hit immediately. Reread your Freud: that happens at a pre-cognitive, subliminal level. "

CH. "Yes, but Rivka is right, we have to ridicule our enemies, including our interior enemies, our own feelings we hate. I thought of wearing the perfect bob of the corporate businesswoman whom I hate because she gives me inferiority complexes for being so much more accomplished than I and I hate myself for those complexes."

CA.: "You have funny ideas about public relations, dilettantes, both of you! Overkill! The power of persuasion is not only to make others act according to your will, but to make them believe they do it out of their own free will. Make yourself lovable by loving yourself. Christine, with your light blue eyes, you would look lovely in a huge Afro hairdo."

CH.: "The kind I hate when they sit in front of me in a theatre. But, yes, why not blacken whites when whitening blacks is so common—all the plaster-white Michal Jacksons, the blond Beyoncés, Rihannas…"

CA.: "Careful, 'blackface' is now taboo. Instead, you may even do without a wig and defiantly show your bald head—that's even dernier cri. For my work I have to read the society pages. Recently there were quite a few pictures of women without hair in the most gorgeous designer gowns. They do not look like victims. That is real cancer pride. There is also a photo series, 'Scar Project,' by a fashion photographer where women expose the marks of surgery. Caroline of Monaco and Elizabeth Taylor gave photographers permission to take them bald—or did they? I cannot share with you the secrets of my profession but have to admit that sometimes we doctor pictures a bit. Well, my background is fiction."

CH.: "Your background, Cassandra, is classical studies. Wow, that is some quantum jump, from Homer to PR!"

CA.: "Not at all! The common basis of Homer and PR is fiction, or call it 'creative writing,' that sounds more hip. There is not a single element that a modern publicist cold not have learned from Homer:

Agamemnon was vying for supreme reign over all the little kingdoms of the archipelago. How did he lobby? The top model, indispensable for all publicity, was given, Helen, queen of austere Sparta who—conveniently for the project—had just eloped with sexy Paris, son of king Priam of Troy, towards the lascivious luxury of Asia Minor. Respectable justification of the invasion: solidarity demanded of the Greeks to save the honour of one of theirs, Menelaos, cuckolded husband and king of Sparta. So, Agamemnon did not even have to mention the real purpose, the gold of Troy and its habitants turned into slaves, in order to obtain the consensus to revenge Menelaos. At the beginning, the confederate armies had some problem with renewable energy, the wind for their sails. But Agamemnon negotiated with a high-placed personality and decision maker, Poseidon, god of the sea, at great human cost. And the stupid Trojans opened the gate of the citadel to let the wooden horse enter. And how had I, Cassandra, warned them! Apart from modern technology, there is no difference between Agamemnon's strategy and that of a contemporary PR firm. But, Christine, you haven't told us about your profession?"

CH.: "My profession? I am a failed classical ballerina, a failed academic, a failed mother, a failed…"

CA.: "You are going to stop that right away, Christine, even if exhibitionist depression is almost as fashionable as breast cancer. That's just another *coquetterie* on your part."

R.: "May I introduce a conciliatory motion? We are much more fraternally, oh, again!—let's say 'sororely' —united when talking about wigs than about the existential tragedy of depression. So, let's cultivate serenity even in tragic circumstances and their *seemingly* less tragic side effects: we lose not only the hair on our heads but also our brows, lashes and pubic hair."

CA.: "Here, for once I'll honour my name as prophetress of catastrophies. Do you know how to apply artificial lashes or extensions? One by one only, not the whole two ranges sold at the supermarket! Imagine a romantic dinner and the lashes from one eye fall into your – or his – wine glass! Or on the cheese of his *gratin de fruits de mer*! Still worse, imagine a delicate oral work and suddenly there is a mustachoed penis!"

"Ladies, ladies, not so loud! Our visitors must respect the tranquillity of our patients. These are *cancer* patients here!"

A sweet little old lady resembling a white mouse had entered, her frail paw raised in alarm. She was one of the volunteers or 'facilitators' you encounter in major hospitals, as touching in their good will as they are confused when it comes to practical information. You ask about the location of restrooms? They'll send you directly to the emergency room.

Thanks to her, though, we suddenly realized that we had by far exceeded our prescribed twenty minutes of recovery. We had felt so good together. The three graces of ABCV gave themselves a date for aquatic exercises at the Feel Good Center among the bubbles of the Jacuzzi. Cassandra served us more good news: there would be more bubbles afterwards, those of champagne, compliment of her firm Highlife Marketing at the bar of the Sky above the Highline.

Before our departure, stickers were glued on us, warning New Yorkers in the street that we would be radioactive for five hours. I wanted to know why we had to be radioactive in the first place.

"The nuclear test is an affair of the heart," all-knowing Cassandra informed me.

History Repeats

itself as Farce

My name is Karl Marx, and I have more reasons than anyone to be surprised by what seems a new American Revolution.

Granted, there remains my notion of *class struggle.*

But among which classes? Those opposed in my *Communist Manifesto*?

Everything is topsy-turvy.

Ach, *Das Kapital!*

After the paradoxical victory of the American super-capitalist as *vox populi*, I feel betrayed by the very class to which I have dedicated my life, the exploited and humiliated ones, those whom I urged *Workers of the World, Unite!* in the fight against the political and economic *superstructure.*

My *surplus-value theory*, they misinterpret as a mere interest rate concern!

During the electoral campaign, thanks to the ubiquity and invisibility of the ghost and his immunity against the thick coal pollution, I slipped into a pub on the Rust Belt where the guys, behind their huge drafts, were listening to the republican candidate on TV, heads nodding approvingly.

"She's a liar, I'm telling you! She's a liar! With her mouth, with her e-mails, even the classified ones! She is the sweetheart of Wall Street. The Democrats are manipulating at your expense, you, the excluded ones, making the rich richer and the poor poorer."

I can't believe it! Those uneducated reactionary blockheads are quoting *me in support of their cause!*

—That is it! Exactly! He says things like they are. He also knows that a man without a gun is not a man. Me, if they take my gun away from me, I shoot.

—Yes, he is one of us, he understands us and is going to stop all this bugging our factories and coal mines, just because of that Chinese hoax of climate change.

—And our farms! What do those city slickers and animal right freaks understand about hogs? Joe, do you 'love and respect' each of your thousand sows?

(Loud laughter)

—And Pete, do you love and respect each of your thousand laying hens?

—No, but that other chick, hopefully our next first

lady, that one, I'd gladly lay. With 'love and respect.'

Much beer was spilled when cheering that idea.

"You who work honestly and pay your taxes, they don't give a damn about you. At the heart of the country, from the Mid-West to our Southern borders, you are losing your jobs under the savage invasion of Mexicans who steal your smartphones and rape your daughters. The factories where you made a living are going to rust and reborn in China."

—Each of us is going to lose his house, his car, his pants to all these immigrants pampered by our 'compassionate' government.

—And to lose our minds! He drives me nuts, that fellow that yells all the time from his mini…mini…, well, his tower, to call to the fight against law-abiding, church-going Christians. I tell you, a Muslim is someone who believes in Islam and someone who believes in Islam is a terrorist—or a Marxist, that comes to the same.

Oh, my God! No, I cannot invoke God, having taught that *religion is opium for the people*.

Yet, after all, it wouldn't hurt the Bible Belt to become a little bit doped, less fanatic about abortion and less parochial. Did the people really forget about the *Internationale*, did even the Proletariat I counted upon forget it?

A ghost moves faster than jets and the helicopters toward their landing pads on Trump this, Trump that building across the continent. So, later in the evening of the memorable post-election day, I offered myself a stroll through Manhattan's southern Central Park area which is so representative of educated, urban America and "insane money": the liberal, self-righteous ones, in other words, those who—at least pretend to—advocate my ideas. I would never have thought that those now mocked as old-fashioned *68ers* or *limousine socialists*, that is, pseudo-socialists, the self-declared "progressives" would be the last defendants of my nineteenth-century thought.

The dog owners among them meet every morning around the Central Park ball fields before mandatory leash law, coming out of buildings such as Trump International Tower or the Plaza.

In contrast to their happily frolicking dogs, the masters appeared like beaten dogs, heads hanging down, no longer masters of their destiny.

—Shell shocked! Catastrophe! A revolution is

needed! We must change the Constitution. Not only abolish the Second Amendment but the Electoral College.

—That xenophobic, lecherous, vulgar, racist, sexist!

—He will destroy the planet with his festival of drilling, fracking, mining, clear-cutting forests and the extinction of species. The Donald named as the head of the Environmental Protection Agency the CEO of an oil company and other foxes as guardians of the respective chicken coops. EPA becomes PPA, the Polluters' Protection Agency. Of course, he will abandon the Paris Agreement on Climate Change. Poor planet!

—If it were only the planet that would be annihilated! What about our values, our culture, our tradition of hospitality?

—Everything is going to be brought down to the level of those Hillbillies, the blue-collar white trash. There, you have it, our new superstructure!

Superstructure! Well, at least they read me!

Those, of course had to in college, Sociology 101, while the Hillbillies only read the sports-sex-crime tabloids.

With some Schadenfreude I realize that theelite gathering here on the dog playground, the "progressives," are still spooked by the *Spectre of Communism* which my enemy, McCarthy, plagiarized from my Manifesto.

When I lived in my shabby hotel in Paris, there was no gauche caviar, no bourgeois-bohème ("bobo") who could have propagated my theories. Even today, it escapes me how they accommodate their (my) ideology with their hedge funds and fiscal paradises among the reptiles of the Cayman Islands.

After all, I shouldn't complain.

Didn't I subscribe to my fellow German Nietzsche's battle cry to "revaluate all values"?

Following the advice of Martin Luther—no, not that one, not the King, I mean the original German reformer, *"man muss dem Volk aufs Maul schauen,"* (one must look at the snout of the people), I flowed down two blocks on Fifth Avenue, in front of Trump Tower, the president elect's residence.

Only an immaterial being—forget *dialectic materialism*—would be able to fight its way through the pandemonium of armies of police and low-flying helicopters that do not manage to control the frenzied masses of *pro* and *con* demonstrators, excited tourists, and warring couples. I overheard:

—You voted for Hillary? I divorce.

—Invite your sister's family for Christmas? No way! Those bastards voted for Trump. I'll never talk to them anymore.

—Did you say this is the victory of the "white trash"? Why do you stress "white"? Do you mean that, normally, only Blacks can be trash? Go to hell, you racist!

I see: This is meteoric—a Continental Divide.

As I always said, history repeats itself as farce. This time, it is not a second *American Revolution*, it is the second *Civil War*.

Ja, ja, my *Klassenkampf* turns into *Rassenkampf*

Note from the scribe: This is a *Mémoire d'Outre-Tombe* of Karl, my compatriot from Rhineland-Palatinate, who will forgive give me for its unauthorized publication.

*The following Essay was first published
in French in the journal* Passages, *Paris.*

Petite-Bourgeois

Swastika

Some twenty years ago a book appeared in Germany, *Die Pfalz unterm Hakenkreuz* (Palatinate under the Swastika)(*1), which presents my native province as a reduced model of the genesis of the Nazi cancer, of the seizure and consolidation of its power, the reaction of the population and the churches, the persecution and "emigration" (read "flight") of the Jews.

Under the editorship of two historians, some dozen contributors draw on local chronicles, most of which were brought to light as late as during the nineteen-eighties and are not available in translation.

This belated appearance is in itself symptomatic of the tendency of us Palatinates to repress, rather than face their past with a view to the much called-for *Vergangenheitsbewältigung* (coming to terms with the past).

This reading was a shock to me.

My south-western province on the left bank of the Rhine (today the Land *Rheinland Pfalz*), then united into a *"Gau"* with the Saarland and thus bordering France, was a fiefdom of Nazism from its first rabble-rousing beginnings in the 1920s.

Of all the provinces of the Weimar Republic, it was Palatinate which supplied, proportionately to the number of its habitants, the largest contingent of members of the NSDAP (*National Sozialistische Deutsche Arbeiterpartei*, in short, Nazi Party): 46 %. Among the towns, my small hometown—Neustadt-an-der-Weinstrasse—distinguished itself still further with its 52%.

In urban areas the members were predominantly small business owners, in rural zones they were mostly elementary school teachers and small wine growers.

One partial explanation for the party's particular hold in this region is the violent resentment of a population humiliated by the Treaty of Versailles, a feeling exacerbated in Palatinate by the reintegration into France of Alsace-Lorraine, which turned Palatinate into a forgotten *Grenzland* (border province).

Remembrance of Things Cursed.

From that dim zone of the mind, where memories of early childhood, stories later heard, and photographs superimpose themselves as on a thrice exposed negative, some faces emerge: There was the sinister *Gauleiter* (governor of the province), Joseph Bürckel, rival of Himmler in the competition for Hitler's favors. An anti-Semite zealot, he became *Reichskommissar* for the "reunification" of Austria with the German Reich (1938, *Anschluss*). The propaganda drew its references usually from more mythical than historical Middle Ages; this "reunification" played on the notion of some Holy Roman Empire of German Nation. In 1940 Bürckel sent a telegram to Hitler boasting his province as the first *"judenfreie Gau"* (free of Jews). This village teacher and local journalist, son of a baker, co-founded in 1926 the bi-monthly journal *Der Eisenhammer* (the iron hammer or anvil)—always this martial-mythical reference to heroes of medieval Germanic lore, especially revived by Wagner's operas, here to Siegfried of the *Nibelungs* and the anvil. Bürckel's journalistic experience taught him that, for the publicity of his thundering harangues on Neustadt's marketplace, his grandiose staging of nocturnal processions around the historical Maxburg fortress (*2), lit by a thousand torches symbolizing the thousand years of the Reich, as well as for the *Parteitage* (party celebrations) in Nuremberg, he needed my father, a renowned photographer.

In order to win over this reluctant, apolitical artist, he frequently stopped for a visit at our house, number 5 of the former "Town-Wall Street" whose name had been recently changed into "Joseph-Bürckel Strasse." This is where the studio 'Photo Gerspach' was founded by my grandfather in 1897. It documented the local history through pictures, first salt prints, then silver prints and finally Leica pictures for the newspapers, and, from the thirties on, through films. By its portrait studio, Photo Gerspach was intimately woven into the private lives of virtually every family in town and surrounding areas—from the cradle to the tomb—through the ritual of portraits of naked babies on a polar bear hide, catholic communions, protestant confirmations, soldiers in their first uniform, marriages, funerals. Only the funerals were shot on location at the cemetery; all the other milestones of life were foiled by one of four backdrops to choose from: a pastoral landscape, the *Neuschwanstein* castle, a rose garden, and a grape-harvesting scene. As an establishment, Photo Gerspach was, therefore, indispensable as media support of a propaganda seeking its collaborators systematically among people well integrated into the local milieu.

During his visits, Bürckel always asked to play with me. Riding on his back, I called him "Dicker Bär" (fat bear, a fitting epithet). So he brought me a brown teddy bear, adorable with its black-on-white swastika on a red brassard, from Nuremberg, the city famous for its cute mechanical toys and the *Judengesetze* (the sinister 1935 laws governing the status of Jews), the triumphant *Parteitage* parades, as well as for the tragic fall of the god-like "heroes" at the post-war Nuremberg trials. Bürckel's seemingly unpretentious joviality and local dialect pleased the good people. The convivial bliss reached its peak during buddy Hermann's visits. Göring's glutton baby face was beaming with beatitude behind his *Schoppen* of golden Palatinate wine at the village fairs.

My father, with his Percival-like naïve sense of friendship and camaraderie, did not wish to be perceived as *"Querulant,"* a Nazi term used in a semantic gradation stretching from simple "glum and nagging spoil sport," to *Volksfeind,* "enemy of the people," or, at least "ungrateful." Hadn't our Führer given us an unprecedented economic boom, work for everybody after the quagmire of the Weimar Republic? Hadn't he given us *Autobahnen* and the Volkswagen to drive on them according to the principle of *Kraft durch Freude* (pleasure as source of energy), an energy fueling the German athletes to victory in the 1936 Olympic Games in Berlin? And with all those spectacular military marches and mass celebrations amidst Albert Speer's Caesarean architecture, was he not an authentic Caesar giving us *panem et circenses*—as all dictators cater to the people's lust for circuses.

The epithet *"Volksfeind"* was dangerous, of course. Hitler had warned: *"Wer nicht für mich ist, ist gegen mich"* (he who is not for me is against me). Characteristic of totalitarianism, he went well beyond the *"état c'est moi"* (the state is me) of French royal absolutism which implies only norms of public behavior.

Totalitarianism, in contrast, targets the totality of the individual, the most intimate life and ways of thinking, feeling, and believing of every citizen. Not content with domination through concrete coercion, the Führer wanted to dominate desire: "Der *Volkswillen bin ich.*" (The will of the people is me.)

As early as 1936, execution announcements were posted on walls everywhere, reporting in detail the misdeeds of the hapless enemies of the people. A psychosis of culpability seized the population. The humblest street sweeper felt guilty of things whose meaning he did not even grasp.

Any form of meeting, such as my mother's *Kaffeeklatsch* (ladies meeting for pastry and chats in the café) or my father's bowling club became suspicious as potential centers of conspiracy. People internalized such suspicions: hadn't one perhaps made a remark that other evening? The psychosis of the ruled and the paranoia of the ruler reflected and enhanced each other.

Bürckel imposed the installation of the daily newspaper NSZ *(National Sozialistische Zeitung)*, the Party's official organ, in the *bel-étage* of our house, conveniently housing together editorial office and photographic support.

My father, naturally, had been granted the *Ariernachweis* (certification of at least four generations of pure Aryan descent); he was not known as "*Bolschewik*," i.e., communist; he did not figure on the list of producers of "*entartete Kunst*," (degenerate, experimental art, not conveying the propaganda values of national-socialist realism), nor was he a "Separatist" (member of the movement for making Palatinate a part of France). With so many positive qualities, he had to become a party member. He did so under pressure from Bürckel, while the majority of Neustadt's inhabitants joined the Party by sincere enthusiasm, by opportunism, or by cowardice in varying proportions. Soon, however, he fell into disgrace. Invited, that is, ordered by Bürckel, to become assistant to Hitler's personal photographer Hans Hoffmann at the *Berghof Adlerhorst* ("Eagle's Nest," Hitler's private alpine retreat near Berchtesgaden), he brought back from this journey mostly pictures celebrating the beauty of the Bavarian Alps rather than that of Hitler, whose portraits he was supposed to make as "Aryan" as possible: back-lit, so as to give blonde tips to the hair, surrounding the bland face with a mythical halo. "I am a national-socialist realist," my father said tongue-in-cheek, "I gave him the Balkan face he really has" (the racist term "Balkan face" referred to any eastern European "gypsy" type).

"You are a sentimentalist, Arthur, a *Schlappschwanz*," barked Bürckel (the extremely vulgar term means "a soft dick"), "and your films don't capture the glory of the military parades and the ecstasy of the crowds cheering their Führer either."

Yet—and this is a telling paradox—Bürckel was himself a sentimentalist in his own fashion. Right after sending hundreds of Jews to Dachau or Auschwitz, tears came to his eyes when listening to a Volkslied, especially the famous *Lindenbaum* (linden tree). Exploiting the emotional effect described by Thomas Mann of this folk song on every German (surpassed only by the *Loreley* whose lyrics, ironically, are by the Jewish poet Heinrich Heine), Hitler ordered "*Hitler linden*" to be planted all over the Reich. Neustadt had already its well-rooted, old *Linde* "near the well outside the town gate", as the song goes. It stood just across the former Town Wall Street, thus facing our house. The smell of its blooms in June is the smell of my childhood.

"I want to see tanks, not little flowers of the meadow," Bürckel kept yelling. "Those are better painted by our Führer." Indeed, the great sentimentalist and failed artist, Adolf Hitler, had produced some quite cute pictures of gentian and Edelweiss, flowers of his native Alps. Alas, they were rejected by the Viennese galleries whose owners were mostly Jewish. *"Ressentiment"* in Nietzsche's sense of the humiliated small chap swearing revenge? Who knows? History might have taken another course, if only one gallery owner had massaged the ego of Adolf, had seen in the bland face the portrait of the artist as a young man. What is certain is that this humiliation taught Hitler that one must play on the individual vanity of those whose adherence one covets.

One example is my uncle Adam—who applied to be called "Baldur," replacing his Hebrew name by that of a Germanic god in reverence to Baldur von Schirach, minister of Youth and Education. Like

Bürckel initially, he was a small village teacher in a giant's body with a bald skull so huge that it could have held far more brain than it did. Promoted SS (*Schutzstaffel*), in his case the modest duty of pushing everybody down to the bomb shelter during air raids, he suddenly saw himself invested, thanks to Hitler, with a power he could never have dreamt of acquiring through his limited talents: the power to instill fear. One must emphasize that, contrarily to certain opinions held abroad, the brown terror exercised itself on the entire population, even on families as "pure-blooded" as mine and most of our employees. My father was accused of having hired two *Mischlinge* (mixed breed, half-Jew, product of *Rassenschande*, the shameful contamination of the race). He was, "luckily," called to the Russian front as war photographer, which spared him the painful choice of either firing his two esteemed co-workers or exposing his family to punishments whose severity no one could predict.

The incessant propaganda was a mix of intimidation on the one hand and that home-grown form of joviality that reassured those still harboring certain moral doubts—the SS (*SchutzStaffel*) and the SA (*Sturmabteilung*) were known for their sense of humor, a quality to which the people of Palatinate are particularly receptive. One may remember the backslapping, hollering *Oberförster* (supreme master of the forest) in Ernst Jünger's novel *The Marble Cliffs*.

Spoken in your native dialect, a veiled menacing statement partly loses its sting. Familiarity is soothing. This populist approach, authority so unpretentious, in the person of a guy just like us, yet unquestionably representing authority, simply ensnarled the populace. The educated ones, especially the shy ones and women in general, conditioned for generations to obedience as the supreme virtue, repressed automatically the occasional spark of revolt.

A scene witnessed from her window kept haunting my mother till the end of her days: the house slipper lost by an old man running in his white night gown along the Joseph-Bürckel Strasse in the freezing early morning hours after the *Kristallnacht* in November 1938, during which Neustadt's synagogue and the Jewish old people's home were set on fire. ("Crystal night" is a sadistic euphemism, evoking a lavish celebration, champagne flowing into precious crystal flutes. There was more harm done than the smashing of the glass window fronts of Jewish stores.) My mother ran downstairs to open the door to the shivering, confused old man. But she already heard the cracking noise of Adam's high leather boots in the entrance hall. He caught her by the shoulders: "*Sei brav, Hildchen, mach keine Dummheiten. Das sind ja keine Menschen, das sind doch Untermenschen!*" (Be a good girl, my little Hilde, don't do foolish things. These are not humans, these are sub-humans.) Fatherly, tender warning to a child set upon playing with a dangerous object. Primary meaning intended: a dangerous toy, a Jew. Implied meaning: I, Adam-Baldur, was witness. My mother melted into tears. That was all she was able to do. Then she went up and sat down at the piano to play Grieg. That was her form of "inner emigration."

It would be too facile for me to say post factum that, in her place, I would have scratched Adam's eyes out with my nails, bitten the aorta at his throat, kicked him in the place where it hurts the macho most, anything, to push my way to the street and the old man. But I never lived consciously under totalitarianism. Hitler, helped by his Propaganda Minister Goebbels, had too well put to his use the legendary German *Obrigkeitshörigkeit* (traditional obedience to authority by the *Untertan* (subject) of the Kaiser (we remember Heinrich Mann's satiric novel). Two centuries earlier, even Schiller, tame after his stormy revolutionary youth, praised that virtue in earnest in his poem "The Dragon killer" where the hero is reminded by monastic authority that *"Mut zeiget auch der Mameluk /Gehorsam ist des Christen Schmuck"* (Courage is shown also by the Muslim/ Obedience is the Christian's glory.) Or was Schiller really so serious when agreeing with the abbot? As serious as Voltaire when exhorting us to aspire at nothing more than taking care of our own garden?

Authority was anybody representing the state, which, corresponds to Hegel's arguable conviction that "the state is the only possible space for the development of the highest possible *Sittlichkeit* (virtue, moral value)." Few women of my mother's generation and before would have braved authority. Authority was sacred, even when incarnated by an imbecile brute. There was nowhere an appeal to critical thought. My mother was held back by that *Pflichtbewusstsein* (conscience of duty) which Kant, arguably too, had raised to the rank of "the only authentic freedom." Take that freedom one step further, and you have the freedom promised on the banner over the entrance to Auschwitz: *"Arbeit macht frei"* (work leads to freedom)

There was only one freedom fighter, hero of the resistance in our house: my maternal grandfather, original forever juvenile, inflamed not by the Nazi journal *Der Stürmer* (storm assault man), but by *Sturm und Drang* (storm and passion), the 18th.-century romantic literary-revolutionary movement as represented by... indeed ... Schiller's *The Brigands* and *Wilhelm Tell*.

As soon as the sirens howled announcing one of the increasingly frequent air raids, and Adam pushed everybody toward the basement, grandfather, with his Stentor's voice, began to sing the Marseillaise: *"Allons, enfants de la patrie...contre la tyrannie!"* "Tiranniiié" I echoed, excitedly jumping in rhythm from the potato heap to the coal heap and back. *"Führerbeleidigung!"* (offense to the Führer) howled Adam over the howling of the sirens. "If that old fool is too vigorous, we can always do a little bloodletting."

The following week, his food distribution coupons were refused to my grandfather.

Ah, how exciting were those nights in the basement for us children. Our cellar being the largest and deepest, still protected in part by remainders of the twelfth-century town wall, it was the assigned bomb shelter for the immediate neighbors, too. A super sleep-over. The grown-ups behaved in such funny ways, passing from hysterical laughter to screams of panic, from gallows humor to sonorous sobbing, whenever the thick stone walls trembled and rocked. They uncorked, one after the other, the best bottles of wine, those which had not yet been bartered against eggs, flower, or butter from nearby small farms. My thirteen-year old "big cousin" whom I greatly admired because of her BDM (*Bund deutscher Mädchen*, union of German girls) jacket with its brown leather buttons, did her homework by reciting the Horst Wessel Lied and others contained in her schoolbook, where nothing else could be found but drawings of Hitler and the HJ (*Hitlerjugend*, Hitler Youth, the corresponding organization for boys), plus a mind-numbing repetition of "*Heil Hitler*" and "*Unser Führer.*" The Führer put all his hopes in a thus indoctrinated youth, which did not prevent my cousin from sticking out her tongue to Adam—who ignored it. After all, she was young, blond, blue-eyed…

The assembly was completed by two hens whom everybody implored not to cackle in Adam's presence, because all "*kriegswichtige Kleinvieh*" (war-important small backyard life stock) was requisitioned by the Party. Even more compromising was the presence of two "*Bolschewiks,*" factory workers of the IG Farben Industry of nearby Ludwighafen, who ignored the end-result of their work intended by superior IG echelons: Cyclon B, the gas used in the showers of concentration camps. Together with the BASF of Mannheim just across the Rhine, IG Farben lent provincial Neustadt its status as primary target of allied bombers.

One evening, Adam-Baldur arrived at an unusual hour. "Im Namen des Führers!" In the fearful silence a few arms went up for a limp *Heil Hitler. Die deutsche Wehrmacht hat einen neuen Triumph.*

That moment was chosen by one of the hens to announce triumphantly that she had laid an egg. My cousin puffed out with laughter so contagious that nobody was able to hold back. Adam pulled out his pistol and, after a second of immobility facing us, turned on his heels and, head high and stiff with scorn, moved to the cellar door where he bumped his head at the low stone frame. The next day a violet bulb had grown on his forehead.

My mother, although deprived of her piano, had been the calmest of them all until a jar of her strawberry-rhubarb jam fell from its shelf, shaken by the bomb that exploded the neighboring house. The jar exploded on the stone floor. My mother wept. She had been busying herself sewing an apron for me from the only material available to the citizens of the Thousand-Year Reich, the red canvas of the Nazi flag from which the white circle with the black swastika had been carefully cut out. Since one had to hoist the flag at every glorious occasion - and there were only glorious occasions - and since one was pressured into proving one's patriotism by buying more flags than one had windows to hang them from, all our clothing had that same origin, with one exception in my case: I was the proud owner of a vaporous white summer dress made of parachute silk from an allied plane shot down over my grandfather's vineyards.

One night in the cellar, we found that, by a mistake of his mother sewing in the obligatory semi-obscurity, the buttocks of our little neighbor Gerhard were signed by a black-on-white swastika. His pants were taken off hastily when Adam's boots were heard cracking on the cellar stairs. The two *Mischlinge* were no longer with us. They had "moved" for better work opportunities elsewhere. *Arbeit macht frei.*

Jewish cosmopolitanism and the good people of our town.

At the beginning of the twentieth century, ten thousand Jews (one and a half percent of the population) lived in Palatinate. They were 7850 in 1925; 6487 in 1933; 4229 in 1937 (*3). Sixty percent were merchants; the remainder, mostly urban, were doctors, journalists, lawyers, merchants, intellectuals, all very respected in their fields, until their propensity towards "bolschevik" left-wing radicalism was discovered - or invented. In contrast, the rural "cattle Jew" or wine dealer was the joy of caricaturists.

By her geographical proximity, France was initially the obvious choice for emigrating Palatinate Jews. Emigration was a particularly painful option for them. Few families were as rooted in the Rhine/Palatinate region as were some Jewish ones (*4) In their own perception, these twentieth-century Jews were so utterly German that they could not think of another *Heimat* (home province). That proved fatal: many made up their mind too late, after the Jew Léon Blum was succeeded as president of France by a Daladier eager to practice appeasement with Hitler. Or they were unable to pay the "emigration tax," a cruel irony. Those who did reach France evenually ended up at Oloron-Sainte-Marie at the foot of the Pyrenees in the Gurs camp. Then Drancy, then...

There had lived in Neustadt a Mr. Lilienhain (literal German meaning: valley of lilies) whom I know only from local lore, because he left before I was born. He used to be the prosperous and immensely popular owner of Neustadt's only department store, the ladies' paradise. He was the first in his business to introduce Parisian fashion (some copied in his own workshop after patterns bought in Paris) and other unheard-of innovations, such as fashion shows modeling pretty local girls on the catwalk (the ambition to be a "Lilienhain girl" engendered dream and drama), and his café—a café in a department store?!—served the best pastry in town at prices far below those of the other cafés. At my father's question how he did it, he laughed: "Of course, Arthur, the café operates at a deficit. But in order to hold their *Kaffeeklatsch* there, the ladies have to pass through the entire store. Now do you know any woman capable of going through a department store without buying anything at all?"

So popular Mr. Lilyofthevalley was that his fans, including the members of my mother's *Kaffeeklatsch*, put a huge arrangement of lilies-of-the valley in front of the store entrance for his birthday on May first and sang a Happy Birthday song to the sound of small bells (the German name of the flower is *Maiglöckchen*, May bells).

But one day, Mr. Lilienhain and his family had "moved." Nobody knew where to nor why he had been in such a hurry to sell both his house and his store. The butcher who bought his house bragged of an excellent bargain. His so far frustrated competitor in ladies' apparel bought the store. But the ladies deplored the disappearance, with Mr. Lilienhain, of the wind of the wide world. Neustadt was cleaned of "Jewish cosmopolitanism."

Jewish cosmopolitanism, a superiority dimly perceived by the provincials and all the more irritating as it could not easily be pinned down, bothered the small business owner who saw his inferiority proven black-on-white - or even in red - on his ledger; it bothered the small journalist confined to the "local events" column; the subtlety of "Talmudic argumentation" bothered the adverse lawyer; the proverbial Jewish sense of money bothered the holder of a modest savings account booklet where the assets had melted during the Depression. Depression, of course, had to be attributed to the international Jewish conspiracy, alternately "capitalist" and "Marxist."

Oxymora, such as capitalist-Marxist, were by no means rare. The painter Hitler knew how to gum colors. Those slogans, precisely because of their lack of logic—or meaning altogether—escaped any objective refutation while stirring some layer of the unconscious in the mass psyche. Hitler's mastery of the guru discourse, i.e., dissolving logical contradictions and incompatibilities in a luminous mist, explains at least in part the striking phenomenon of his uniting under the swastika banner and within the "National Socialist German Workers Party" such strange bedfellows as the industry barons of the Ruhr, Prussian heel-clicking Junkers, almost all the petty-bourgeoisie and, indeed, the factory workers.

There were plenty of examples of such logical prestidigitation following the same scheme: starting with a lie which consists precisely of calling "lie" the truth expressed by somebody one wants to harm, one can trigger the cog-wheels of a circular "logic." Propaganda Minister Goebbels: "Absurd rumors are being spread abroad of horrendous crimes committed against German Jews. As always, at the root of the lies is the international Jewish conspiracy. The German Jews who, obviously, initiated this slander campaign against the Reich, will have to pay from now on. They have only themselves to blame for the troubles ahead of them." Propaganda, however, was able in rare cases only to engender genuine hatred against an individual. Few people saw a reason for scorning suddenly those with whom they had been rubbing elbows in the streets, cafés, and *Weinstuben* of the small town. But like someone whose chances of promotion are menaced by the presence of a brilliant colleague would not be displeased to see him leave, people avoided pondering too much about the circumstances.

One could have known, to be sure, by making a small effort. But no immediate evidence compelled one to make that effort. There was no KZ (concentration camp) in Neustadt's surroundings. Nothing spoilt the picturesque chain of villages strung along the vineyard hills bordering the *Weinstrasse* (Wine Road) that stretches toward Alsace and the famous *Weintor* (Wine Gate), a Caesarean triumphal arch, pompously inaugurated in 1935 by Bürckel surrounded by pretty maidens in folkloric dresses. Why not, then, enjoy it all, draw *Kraft through Freude* (strength through joy) instead of calling for trouble. Thanks to the childish passion for eavesdropping, I still remember a conversation among the "sisters" of my mother's *Kaffeeklatsch* about an absentee one: "*Die Liesel ist doch eine Wüste, die laden wir nicht mehr ein*" (Liesel is really unpleasant, let's not invite her anymore)."She can't help coming up with those horror stories about concentration camps and little children killed. She has a macabre imagination. Still, I cannot sleep the night after." "She should have enough tact not to offend other people's sensibility." "Anyhow, this is not the occasion; we come together to have fun and cake. The times are dark enough." "What could we do anyhow?"

Who will throw the first stone? I am often asked to be "polite" and respect other people's feelings when I cannot help coming up with horror stories about child abuse or cruelty to animals going on virtually under our eyes - if only we choose not to turn them away - in this very city, civilized and compassionate New York. Yet, here, if we wanted to "do something," we would not risk our lives. "I have no opinion," said our cleaning woman in Neutadt. "If I had one, they'd punish me."

There were, however, those who refused that ostrich policy. In Palatinate at least, the Catholic church played a more positive role than the Protestant one. As a result, several priests, who had revolted against the new paganism of Rosenberg or the juxtaposition of the Cross of Jesus with the *Hakenkreuz* (swastika cross) ended up in Dachau. The simple, but clear-sighted and deeply Catholic mother of Bürckel himself pleaded with her son: "Ach, Seppl, *mach's doch nicht so schlimm!*" (My little Joe, don't be so bad). She succeeded in saving several people, but when she began to become embarrassing to her son, he declared that one should not pay attention to the babble of an old hag.

Once Germany was essentially "judenfrei," Hitler started hating the "blacks" (Catholics). Even a lesser crime than hiding a Jew could send you to Dachau: a hunter joked that the boars at the time he was mayor were black and now they were brown (color of the Nazi uniform).

The SS, phalanx for the protection of the people, was fast in taking care of this enemy of the people.

He was led away the very next day.

The Angel of the Apocalypse.

Then came the time of the gas masks and the haggard masses from the East, fleeing the advance of the Russians. Still the radio's triumphant *Sondermeldungen* (special announcements) with their ritual fanfare openings ceaselessly informed us of new victories. Although our area was one of the last where the *Flak* (German air defense) was still shooting down *Jabos* (*Jagdbomber*, allied bomber fighter planes), there were more and more people who had "never been Nazis." March 1945 marked the beginning of gruesome settlings of accounts. Adam was beaten with a ferocity that left him invalid for the short remainder of his life. At the "denazification" period after the end of the war, his widow asked for—and obtained—his posthumous status as "victim of fascism," because he had committed his deeds only under coercion from his superiors (*Obrigkeitsgehorsam* !) and had paid with his life for not being powerful enough to resist. A posthumous irony for someone so much enjoying his pathetically small crumb of power. Bürckel escaped denazification by dying in October 44 under mysterious circumstances. A rumor had it, he died under delirium tremens. But was not the whole period a collective delirium tremens?

Out of fear that the American occupant might find compromising objects, one burned pell-mell all "Hitleriana," which, by yet another sinister irony, would fetch millions of dollars on today's collector's market in America. The water of my baths was heated by thousands of Hitler postcards. The celluloid of the films of the Nuremberg *Parteitage,* catching fire together at once, made our kitchen stove explode.

One day I saw an angel from our kitchen window. "Mommy, come here, an angel all in flames!" "The angel of the Apocalypse," my mother murmured, "It's an English *Jabo* shot down by the *Flak.*" "Will the angel die? But...he is bad, isn't he, he is English?" (The words "Americans," Russians," "English" were automatically preceded by "*böse*", bad, a fixed epithet). "Why?...Oh, yes...No...I don't know...But somewhere there will be a mommy crying."

Why-oh yes-no-I don't know...I still try to decipher the letters my father sent from the front. Laborious endeavor, because I have never learnt the supposedly

"Germanic" gothic writing imposed by Hitler. The letters speak of his love for us, of his nostalgia for his native soil. *Heimat*, the native soil, the romantic setting that nourished the imagination of the child I was with fairy tales, with lieder; that through which my parents have opened my receptivity to the beauty of the native woods and vineyards and the poetry chanting them – this soil should harbor the roots of Nazism? Is that the *Boden* , *blutig* , *völkisch?*

The microcosm of Neustadt is revealing: fascism is not primarily the affair of warlords. The Caesarism of a dictator of a thousand-year Reich needs millions of smallnesses to make him stand upright: petty bourgeois, petty officials, petty merchants with their petty jealousies and vengeful desires. These are the "resentments of the flies of the market place," but which, far from gnawing at grandeur of the superman, as seen by Nietzsche, project upon him their libido to the point of merging with his person, relinquishing all individual judgment and moral conscience, a phenomenon described by Freud in his *Psychology of the Masses.* Those *Mitläufer* (hangers-on) bathe in a reflected glory that is all the more radiant, as it is minutely programmed to this effect. From a certain moment on, the mass of people, small and meek under ordinary circumstances, may turn into a multi-headed, blood-thirsty beast.

All this took place in the shadow of a gothic church (thirteen-century gothic, but no more "Germanic" for that than Chartres or Burgos), amidst that *Gemütlichkeit* (cozy, warm, intimate atmosphere, reassuring by its familiarity) of the romantic little town with its gabled houses and crooked medieval streets. It took place far from such capitals as Berlin and Munich with their grandiose parades of tanks and army columns; far from the Krupps and other Ruhr barons who had an obvious interest in militarization; far from the Prussian aristocrats and their clicking spurs. It took place among the good people of the native soil. It was grotesque, but in the sense of that word as used by Freud as a version of *"unheimlich"* (uncanny), that is, of an ugliness which would be ridiculous, were it not at the same time obscurely menacing. That Freud used for the elaboration of his notion of *Das Unheimliche* (The Uncanny) a tale by the quintessential German romantic poet E.T.A. Hoffmann, *Der Sandmann* (best known to the American public through the ballet *Coppelia* and the opera *Tales of Hoffmann*) is as telling as the fact that, in this particular Hoffmann's tale, the uncanny is not only the grotesque puppet maker Coppelius, but the automaton, the inanimate doll mechanically executing the movements orchestrated by her master, and shattered into pieces at the end. "*Deutschland soll in Blut und Flammen mit mir untergehn*" (Germany must perish with me in blood and flames) Hitler is quoted to have said at the very end.

An *unheimliche*, disquieting otherness had infiltrated the familiar, playing on the very registers of that familiarity of my *Heim* (home), our *Heimat* (native region) to which I remain sentimentally attached. The absolute Evil was hiding under the familiar face of the ordinarily good-natured neighbor turned pillar of the Party. What is uncanny is, to borrow Hannah Arendt's term, *The Banality of Evil.*

Author's Notes start on next page.

Author's Notes

1. Nestler, Gerhard and Ziegler, Hannes, eds. *Die Pfalz unterm* Hakenkreuz, 2nd. ed., Landau, Pfalz: Pfälzische Verlagsanstalt, 1997.

2. Maxburg, named after king Maximilian of Bavaria from the time Palatinate was united with Bavaria. Officially known as the *Hambacher Schloss*, where the *Hambacher Fest* took place in 1832, a sequel to the July Revolution of 1830 in France, mostly inspired by the liberal literary movement *Junges Deutschland* whose main representative is the poet Heinrich Heine.

Hambach is part of the township of Neustadt, which led the townspeople to declare Neustadt as "the cradle of German democracy." In reality, the "historical event" had no practical consequences at all, but was typical of the local spirit: a Fest with lots of wine and exalted talk. It was romantic. If it did lead indirectly to some democratization, then Neustadt will have to admit that it owes this distinction to the Jew Heine. We owe him also that most romantic Volkslied, die *Loreley*. The maiden's rock above the Rhine is part of our local lore. The *Hambacher Fest* did, indeed, trigger the economic insight of Friedrich List who, in his *National System of Political Economy* (1841) asked for common import taxes for the German states. He is thus considered a pioneer of today's European Union.

3. Roland Paul, *"Es war nie Auswanderung, immer nur Flucht"* (it was never emigration but always flight) in Alfred Hans Kuby, ed."J*uden in der Provinz: Beiträge zur Geschichte der Juden in der Pfalz zwischen Emanzipation und Vernichtung."* Neustadt, 1989.

4. One must remember that some of the most eminent figures of the Kabbalah lived in Speyer, Worms and Mainz (the "garlic" towns along the Rhine, their initials forming the Hebrew word *shum*, garlic) already in the twelfth century, as early as their co-religionaries in Southern France (Provence) and Northern Spain, that is, three hundred years before the massive emigration from Spain at the time of the Inquisition.

Jewish presence, however, dates much farther back than medieval Kabbalah. Soldiers from Judaea came as part of Roman regiments to the Rhine.

Acknowledgments

My thanks go to all the usual suspects, such as heroically patient spouses and family members conventionally mentioned last as "last not least."

My friend and editor, William Armitage, deserves my gratitude for his perspicacious advice and draconian pursuit of inappropriate prepositions (English is not my native language).

The technical preparation of the manuscript would have taken much longer without my friend, Ken Benshish, who many times served as a lifesaver to me, the technophobe routinely drowning in a whirlpool of computer complications. Our friendship has its origin in that between our dogs in Central Park where once he saved my dog from drowning in the Lake.

I owe an enriching perception of nature to the poet and installation artist Cecilia Vicuña since I was privileged to work with her on a previous book.

I feel intimately related to many "friends" met virtually or personally and who saved me from depression over the daily news about the dismal treatment we humans inflict on animals. The long list, by no means exhaustive, includes Paul McCartney, Ricky Gervais, Peter Egan, Candice Bergen, Ingrid Newkirk, Couto (against religious animal sacrifice), Brigitte Bardot, Nina Jackel, Jean-Baptiste del Amo, Jonathan Foer, Kitty Block, Brigitte Gothière, Azzedine Downes, and Alex Baldwin, people whose determination allows us to believe that the fight against insensitivity toward those who share this earth and time with us is no longer utopia but reality animating society as a whole.

About the Author

Christine de Lailhacar is of German origin with French/American citizenship. Educated in an advanced German "Gymnasium" school with emphasis on Latin and Greek, she studied Political Science in Paris before earning an MA degree in Political Science from CUNY, New York (Russian Area). She received her Ph.D. in Comparative Literature from Columbia University.

A former associate professor at the State University of New York, she divides her time between Manhattan and the French countryside with her Russian-born husband and her German Shepherd, *Jeira*.

She is a member of the Authors Guild, New York, and the Maison des Ecrivains, Paris. She is also a member of the Comité de Rédaction of the revue "Passages" Paris.

She is the author of *Salt Prints* (a novel) and *The Mestizo as Crucible: Andean Indian and African Poets of Mixed Origin as Possibility of Comparative Poetics*.

She regularly contributes book chapters and articles, writing in German, French, English, Spanish, and Russian.

Salt Prints (Novel)

The love between two individuals in New York of the 1980s and '90s is jeopardized by the centuries-old German-Jewish ambiguity between love and hate, fascination and fear, while it is equally characterized by the traditional mutual fecundation in science and the arts.

Under both comical and tragic circumstances, they cope with the ever-present past, its imprints bitter like the salt prints, earliest grainy photo positives obtained from salted paper they find in Adolf-Eugene's great-grandfather's studio in Worms-on-Rhine.

and...

The Mestizo As Crucible: Andean Indian and African Poets of Mixed Origin as Possibility of Comparative Poetics (Studies in Modern Poetry)

www.ingramcontent.com/pod-product-compliance
Lightning Source LLC
Chambersburg PA
CBHW052142170626
46812CB00004B/1551